ng's Highlander

By

Audrey Harrison

Published by Audrey Harrison

Find more about the author and contact details at the end of this book and the chance to obtain a free copy of The Unwilling Earl.

Proofread and edited by Jenny Warren and can be contacted at jenny@warrenproofreading.co.uk or www.warrenproofreading.co.uk

Cover by Covers and Cupcakes
www.coversandcupcakes.com

Prologue

Captain Avril had never watched someone as closely as he did Alice as she slept. Every movement she made, every time she winced as she turned her head, he moved to the edge of his seat, wanting to go to her but not wishing to cause her pain.

Thoughts were rushing through his mind, tearing at his insides in a way he had not experienced for years, and he was struggling with it.

Constantly cursing himself under his breath, he wanted to leave the room, leave the house and go somewhere he could hide and never see anyone else again, but until he knew she would be well, he could do nothing but sit and wait.

***

Eventually, she yawned and stretched a little, wincing when the lump on her head touched the pillow. Blinking herself awake, she looked in surprise at Captain Avril.

"Have you been tending me?" she asked groggily.

"If you mean, have I been sat here being as helpless as a bairn, yes I have," he replied.

Alice smiled slightly. "You could never be helpless."

"I have certainly felt it this afternoon. What did you think ye were doing, putting yourself against a man three times the size of you?"

"It worked when I stood up to you," she replied.

"That is because I am a gentle soul."

Alice snorted, which made him smile for the first time since she had been carried in. "Could I have some water, please?"

"Oh, yes," he said, standing and pouring a glass. Holding it out to her, he cursed when she tried to sit up unaided and grimaced in pain. "Wait," he commanded. Lifting her gently, he supported her in the crook of his arm and handed her the glass.

Taking the water a sip at a time, Alice revelled in being so close to him. When she had sated her thirst, she tucked her head against his shoulder and closed her eyes with a sigh.

Hearing his sharp intake of breath, she looked up at him. "My head does not hurt when I am like this." She was quite impressed that she could speak, as when she had turned her head to meet his gaze, she had been taken aback by the intensity of his stare. Those blue eyes she had admired from afar were even more impressive up close.

He seemed to be struggling with something, for he did not speak, but he bit his lip. Alice was drawn to the action, and slowly with the hand that was not holding the glass, she reached up and touched his lips.

Her action caused a quiet gasp, but she did not move her fingers away.

"I have longed to do this," she said quietly.

"It is wrong," he said gruffly, but he was watching her with such intensity, she knew he wanted her touch as she wanted to be touched by him.

"Is it? Then I cannot do this?" she asked, running her fingers over his cheek, feeling the stubble that had developed through the day.

Groaning, he moved his hand and mirrored her actions on her cheek. "I thought you were dead," he whispered.

"But I am not. I am here and with you," she replied.

"I should not be doing this," he moaned as he touched his fingers to her lips, which she parted slightly.

"I am glad you are."

"Blast it," he cursed before crushing her to him and taking her mouth to plunder. There was no gentle first kiss for Alice; she had chosen a man who knew what he wanted and gave as much as he took. He teased her, made her breathless, and showed her what it was like to be kissed by a man driven by passion and longing.

Eventually, he pulled away from her, and kissing her forehead, he lay her down on the bed, putting some distance between them.

"Why have you stopped?" Alice asked, afraid of what was to come.

"I cannae do this," he said, hands running through his hair and tugging the ends.

"Kiss me?"

"Oh, I can do that," he said derisively. "It is the falling in love, being with one person, waiting until they let you down, that is what I cannae do."

"That is a huge leap from a kiss," Alice said, trying to inject some humour into the situation.

"But it wasn't, was it?" he demanded of her. "I could have kissed you that first night when you demanded I behaved, as if you were some sort of angry pixie. I have mooned around you like some Johnny Raw since then, and it is not getting any easier."

"I see."

"Is that all you have to say? Have I made you speechless for the first time in your life?"

Alice laughed, despite the knowledge that she was losing him, for she had to. One day she hoped he would be hers, but she knew that now was the wrong time for him. "Never that," she answered. "I am not prepared to argue against nonsensical reasons why we cannot be together when we both know what the real problem is, and until you fix that, you are always going to be troubled."

"And what is that?" he demanded, but he was looking warily at her.

"Until you can face your first love and be sure that she is gone from your heart, there is no room for anyone else," Alice said sadly.

He reared back slightly. "I do not have feelings for her! She betrayed me."

"Yes, you do," Alice insisted. "If you are being honest, you know you do; that is why I have had to wait all this time to receive a single kiss from you. It has been no fun to see you struggling with your feelings, but I know I cannot compete against an image you have in your mind of the perfect woman."

"How can I think she is perfect when she betrayed me?"

"You have blamed yourself for not being there; you do not blame her for her duplicity," Alice said.

Avril hung his head. "I want you. I really do."

"Then go to Scotland and sort out your feelings towards that woman, for I refuse to be second best to anyone."

Glowering at her, he crossed the room, bending to where she was on the pillows and kissed her once, roughly. "You are not second best, but know this, if you meet anyone else whilst I am gone, I will kill him, for I won't be pushed out again."

"Go away, you big oaf," Alice said.

"I mean it."

"And so do I," she said. "I will not have her shadow hanging around for the rest of my days. I want you to be free."

"I do not deserve you."

"Probably not, but we will work on that when you return."

With a smile and a blow of a kiss, he left the room.

Alice closed her eyes for a few moments, tears squeezing out between her eyelashes. She had done the right thing by them both, but it was not an easy thing to do. His first love was married to another, but it did not mean that he would not be affected by her when he was in her company once more.

Cursing herself, she suddenly opened her eyes. “I refuse to just wait until he returns, not knowing what is going on. He needs to exorcise her, but that does not mean I have to be a passive bystander,” she muttered to herself. “No, Alice, it is time to fight for what you want.”

Climbing out of bed, she gingerly walked to her desk, which Lydia had moved to her chamber as soon as they had arrived there to enable her to write in privacy when she wanted to. Sitting down, she closed her eyes for a moment, letting the dizziness pass before moving again.

Pulling the desk drawer open, she took out some paper. “It is time for a journey,” she said to herself. “But I need someone to accompany me. Serena, I hope you are keen for an adventure.” Picking up her quill, she started to write.

Chapter 1

Captain James Avril was a fool. He knew this more forcefully with each mile he travelled on the blasted stage he was crammed into. Not all he had to endure was physical. Being classed as a giant of a man at over six feet in height, broad-shouldered and solid, it was not easy folding himself into such a crowded tight space, but there was more to his turmoil. He had never felt so bereft, well, perhaps once, but he was currently on a journey in which he was sure he had left part of him behind, the wrench felt so real.

His glowers, not aimed at anyone in particular, had persuaded two of the inhabitants of the latest carriage that they would be more comfortable sitting on top rather than face the dark looks of the ogre that was James, muttering curses to himself. The extra room did nothing to relieve him of his present discomfort, for how could it? He felt as if he was being torn in two – literally.

He wanted Alice Boyd, the petite, fiery bluestocking, who could be a termagant one moment and as gentle as a lamb the next. That he knew he was the one to make her flare up made his insides ache, but she could give as good as she got and could certainly stand up to him. He smiled at the thought of their first meeting. He had been in the servants' quarters of her friend Lydia's house, the one she had made a place of respite for those who were homeless or destitute because of the end of the war with the French. He had been in the middle of a battle of wills with the housekeeper who was foolishly trying to relieve him of his kilt.

Stroking the material of the same kilt, which he wore every day, he looked out the window and almost laughed at the memory of Alice walking in with Lydia in the hope that they could achieve what the servants had not. After yet further argument, it was Alice who had berated him and compared him to a bairn, the cheeky minx. When he had dropped his kilt, revealing that in fact he was very much all man, he had expected hysterics, and of course the staff obliged with screams, curses and action to try to cover him up. He had been immune to all that, just watching the pretty bluestocking. He had half expected her to swoon, but she had grinned, her eyes glittering with suppressed laughter. She had looked at her friend, and he could tell they were both trying to contain their amusement from the staff who were ushering them out of the room to protect them from such disgraceful behaviour. If the servants had been in charge, he would have been cast out, but fortunately it was never insisted on by Lydia, so he stayed.

If he was one to believe in love at first sight, he would have been convinced that he had met the woman of his dreams, but experience had taught him that he could not trust such fanciful notions. He had loved once and had been betrayed in the worst possible way. And now he was on his way to face the woman who had broken his heart and the friend who had betrayed him, and all he could think about was that he had left Alice behind.

James had never expected to return home, not after finding out that his betrothed had married his best friend while he was away. He had not anticipated being gone for so long, but military men were needed, and he had wanted to do his duty, and she had promised to wait. It seems she had wanted children and decided that his best friend was a better option to provide them rather than being loyal to her absent betrothed.

Simon had been like a brother to him. They had grown up together, their lands adjoining each other, never a day apart. They had gone to the same school, rode together, chased the girls and fought like only true brothers could. To find that Constance had married Simon was the ultimate betrayal, and James was not sure who had hurt him the most, but it broke something in him.

Already exhausted and overwhelmed by the horrors of Waterloo, the terrible betrayal ignited an uncharacteristic rage in James that could only be assuaged by his fists. Simon offered little resistance, but only when his family stepped in and dragged him away did James stop. Afraid that Simon might perish from the beating, the family tried to send James away for fear he would hang, but he remained in the area until he knew that Simon had survived. He was honourable enough that if he had killed him, he would accept the sentence that would follow. He had not wanted to live at that point, so the prospect of swinging for his crime would not have caused him to run.

When it was clear that Simon would recover, James had a hard decision to make. He loved his family, but he could not bear to be in the same locality as Constance and Simon, so he turned his back on his family and his heritage, presuming he would never return.

What should have happened next was that he met Alice, fell in love, and they lived a contented, uneventful life. Unfortunately, he could never trust any woman after what Constance had done, and although he had every reason to hate her, part of him still clung to what they had shared and how it had felt. She had been his first love, the one he had planned a future with. How could he just switch off his feelings? He was not fickle; when he loved, he loved with his whole heart.

Alice had been the only one since Constance who had made him want a better future, even though he would not allow himself to believe it could happen. Constance had known him for years, accepted his many faults and betrayed him. Why would Alice, a relative stranger, stand by him until their dying day? How could he open himself to the risk of being broken again? There was a whisper inside him that claimed Alice would never do something so cruel, and he thought that with time he might have been willing to take the leap of faith. And then Constance had sent a blasted letter to the place he was staying.

It was a guess on her part. She had clearly seen one of the articles in the newspapers about the new venture Lydia Hesketh was undertaking. He had no idea what Constance had written; he had thrown it in the fire the moment it had been handed to him. But there was no going back, Constance had come back into his life, and it affected everything. Particularly with what could be with Alice.

He smiled as he thought of how she had sent him away. She was a brave little thing, for he knew what her words had cost her. Yes, she had cursed him and demanded that he go and sort out whatever he still felt about Constance, but he could see the sadness she tried to hide. He had told her he would return, but he was not sure she had believed him.

Travelling closer to his beloved Highlands of Scotland, he started to wonder if she knew him better than he knew himself.

***

When James stepped off the final carriage, he stretched and groaned as every part of his body ached. Throwing his bag onto his shoulder, he started the fifteen-mile walk from Aviemore to his home on the outskirts of Grantown-on-Spey. No one was there to meet him, for he had not sent word ahead that he was coming home. If he were being honest with himself, he was not sure what sort of reception he would receive from his family.

He could have easily waved down some farm cart to carry him at least part of the way, but he wanted to walk, to take in the rugged landscape as well as to stretch his legs. As he walked the roads which had been so familiar to him, he almost felt ghostlike, returning to a place he had tried to accept that he would never see again.

The beauty of the Cairngorm mountain range in the distance soothed him as he trudged on. The snow on their tops hinted that winter could be arriving soon and, with it, hard months of living, but it was also the best place to be during the harsh weather. As a child he had been outside whenever the snow had fallen on the lower ground, no matter how cold it was. Playing in the snow was more important than warmth for his friends and himself.

He was disturbed from his reflections by a cart slowing as he walked. “Come home for good, Jimmy?” the gruff voice asked.

James turned to the man, knowing who it was the moment he had spoken. No one else ever called him Jimmy. “I have no idea, Mr MacKinnon,” he replied honestly.

The reply received a nod of understanding. “Aye, but no one blames you for what happened; it was a bad time.”

“It was.” They might live in a very rural area, but news travelled as fast as it did in London.

"Climb aboard," Mr MacKinnon said. "There's no use pondering over what cannae be changed, so the sooner you get home the better."

"I was enjoying the scenery," James defended himself, but he climbed onto the seat next to the old farmer. When given an instruction by such a well-respected elder, you did as you were bid, however large and intimidating you were.

"You looked a million miles away."

"Perhaps not so far, but enough miles for it to hurt," James muttered half to himself. "What have I missed while I've been gone?" He did not wish to go over where he had been and what he had been doing since he left, but he was interested to find out the local news, and Mr MacKinnon knew everyone and everything.

"The usual; bickering, bairns being born and old folks dying," Mr MacKinnon said, chewing on his unlit pipe. "Your da will be glad to see you."

"I am not sure about that. I brought shame on the family."

"You reacted like any other man would have. It was a poor way of paying you back for service to the Crown."

"I could not give two hoots about the Crown," James said. "I just did not want to be forced into learning French if Napoleon invaded." It was more complicated than that, but again James was not about to unburden himself to the old man.

James's words caused a chuckle. "Aye, he was determined to rule the world. He would have got on well with your lass; she wanted the world too."

"She is not mine."

"No, she was foolish in that regard. What made you come back? Though it is good that you are here."

"The past, I suppose, and more importantly, putting it to rest." James did not want to start explaining about Constance's letter or Alice, which would not normally be a problem for him, not being one to divulge anything he did not wish to, but Mr MacKinnon had a way of wheedling information out of a person before they realised they had even spoken.

"Aye, that's always a good thing." They travelled in comfortable silence until they were about two miles from James's family home. "This is where we part, Jimmy," Mr MacKinnon said.

"Thank you for the ride," James said, jumping off the cart, his bag once more flung on his shoulder.

"It was good to see ye, hope to see ye again soon. Dinnae be dragged down by the past; you had a lucky escape there, boy. One day, ye might be thankful for what happened."

With a flick of his wrist, the ever-patient horse started to trundle away once more. James was left staring at the disappearing form of Mr MacKinnon, wondering why he would make such a cryptic comment. Eventually, shrugging his shoulders, he turned towards home.

Chapter 2

James had hardly stepped into the house when he was almost knocked off his feet by the person who had launched herself down the last few stairs and across the hallway with a squeal of delight. Laughing, James swung her into his arms, kissing her cheek as he turned in a circle.

"You came back! Oh, I never thought you would! It is so good to see you! Tell me this is not a dream!" The words were half-laughed, half-sobbed into his neck, where she had tucked herself, clinging to him as if afraid to let him go, lest he disappear.

"Mary, let your brother get inside before he changes his mind and tries to escape from the hoyden you are," the gruff voice of Baron Kirkbride came from the side room that was his study.

Reluctantly letting herself be set down, Mary still clung to James's arm. "Are you here to stay?" she whispered to her brother, worried eyes begging him to answer in the positive. She was very like her brother with strawberry blonde hair and blue eyes, but she was slender and of average height.

"Aye, lass, for a while at least," James said gently before looking at his father. "If that is acceptable, Da?"

"You will always get a welcome here, my boy. I am only sorry you stayed away so long, though I understand why."

"I had determined to never return, and then things changed."

A look of annoyance crossed the baron's face. "Yes, I can imagine what that was. Come, your mother and brothers will be delighted to see you."

James thought the comment from his father was strange, but now was not the time to work out what he could mean, so shrugging his shoulders, he followed his father, Mary still clinging to his arm.

The threesome walked down the wide hallway of the substantial grey granite house that had been in the Avril family for three generations and turned towards the rear of the building. A large, bright room was used as the less formal family room as it had several wide windows, which could take full advantage of the sometimes elusive Scottish sun.

Baron Kirkbride entered the room first. "Sweetling, there is a surprise for you."

James's mother turned at her husband's words and gasped when she saw James standing in the doorway. Needlework was forgotten, tumbling to the floor when she sprang to her feet, and in movements that were only slightly more restrained than his sister's had been, James was enveloped in a tight embrace.

"My boy! My boy! You are well!" she cried over and over.

"I would not go that far, Ma. Have you seen the state of his hair?" came the drawl from the man standing in front of the fire. "And why the devil do you insist on wearing that kilt?" None of the other men wore a kilt, all choosing the more practical breeches.

James smiled at him over his mother's head. "Good to see you, Hamish."

"'Tis good to see you too, brother." Hamish came across to James and slapped him on the back.

A younger boy had been writing in the bay of one of the windows and stood at the commotion James's entrance had caused. When James's mother finally released her tight grip on her son, James looked across at the boy. "This cannae be Drew? He was a little weed when I left; now look at ye, nearly as tall as me."

Drew snorted. "Hardly, but I have grown a foot since you left."

"I hope you are not too big to give your brother a proper welcome," James said, holding his arms open. He smiled when Drew rolled his eyes but walked across the room and was willingly wrapped in his brother's embrace.

"Don't keep a hold of him; he cannae be away from his writing for too long," Mary teased from behind James, making Drew wriggle out of James's arms to glare at his sister.

"At least I'm not mooning over your latest flirt," Drew responded, his scowl very much in competition with any that James was able to produce, though that is where their resemblance ended. Drew looked more like his father, with red hair and green eyes.

"Leave your sister alone," his mother chided. "You know it affects your prose when you are angry."

"Still aspiring to be a writer, eh?" James said. "I know a lady who has written a novel."

"Really? Could I meet her? Would you invite her here? It would be good to be able to speak with someone who understands the torment being unappreciated can be." The last comment was said with another glower towards his sister, enabling James to hide his mixed emotions at Drew's words.

He would like nothing more than to invite Alice here, but he was in no position to raise speculation about why he wanted her near him. He tried to push thoughts of Alice to one side and smiled at his brother. "I am not sure, maybe one day, although I am not aware of any inner torment that she suffered. She always seemed perfectly happy when writing."

Drew sighed. "Then I must carry my burden alone once more." Ignoring Mary's snort of derision, he returned to his desk and, sitting down, turned his back on the family and began to scribble.

James looked around at his remaining family members, a question on his face. His mother smiled indulgently at Drew. "He is convinced that in order to write good poetry, he needs to be a troubled soul. Now come and sit and tell us all that you have been doing while away."

After ordering tea for everyone, they gathered around James as if he was going to tell them some great story. He only gave them a brief overview of what he had been through, leaving out the months he had spent sleeping anywhere he could find a quiet spot. Telling them about Hesketh Hall and everything they were trying to do there was his main focus; he hoped it would convince his family that leaving had been a benefit for him. There was no point worrying them when he was well, it was clear they had concerns enough whilst he was away.

"What a wonderful thing to do. Not everyone would choose to open their home to soldiers," his mother said.

"It was a stipulation in the will, not about the soldiers, but to turn the house into something useful. Miss Hesketh decided it should be for the benefit of the soldiers, and she is just the right person for the task."

"Oooh, is there a romance in the air?" Mary asked eagerly.

James laughed. "No, there is another who has captured that lady's heart."

"Aw, pity. I hoped to have a sister-in-law, but none of you seem willing to marry."

"Mary! Shush! You should not utter such personal remarks; think of James!" her mother chided her, at which the young girl burned with embarrassment.

"I am only sixteen," Drew muttered from the corner. "Allow me a few more years before I have to sacrifice myself to the married state."

"You are ridiculous!" Mary mocked her youngest brother, but his words had lightened the atmosphere. “I am sorry, James, my words were insensitive. I just did not think.”

“Ah, lass, it is in the past,” James said, trying to play down the feelings he had carried with him since his last return.

“Not for us it isn’t,” Hamish said, reaching down to poke the fire, avoiding the daggers his mother sent in his direction.

“What do you mean? How can it affect you?” James asked.

“Nothing,” his mother responded.

“Nay, Ma, I’m no Johnny Raw you can fool. What aren’t you telling me?” When no one responded, James turned to Mary. “What is going on, sister?” He could see that she was bursting to say something and knew she would be the one to give in first.

“She is round here every blasted day!” Mary shot out before shrugging at her mother. “I am not telling any untruths.”

“Constance visits you every day? Why on earth would she do that?” James’s mind was racing. He would have been less surprised to be told that the two families were not speaking to each other; once a breach occurred between families, it usually lasted for years. “What does Simon say to that? Surely, he understands the strangeness of her actions?”

The family looked between themselves before the baron spoke. “Did you not get the letter Constance sent? She was convinced it was the way to find you, and it seems she was right. I presumed that was why you had returned.”

"I threw the letter in the fire the moment I recognised her writing. I never opened it," James said.

"That puts a different perspective on your return," Hamish said with amusement. "I am glad to see you, brother, but I am curious as to why you returned if you had no idea about what has happened?"

"It is complicated," James said but glared at his family. "I hate talking in riddles. Will someone tell me what is going on?"

The baron moved and stood at James's side. Resting his hand on his second son's shoulder, he gave it a squeeze. "Simon is dead."

"What?" James spun around to look at his father before jumping from his seat. "Was it because of the fight? Did I kill him after all? I stayed in the area to be sure; I thought he was well."

Holding up his hands, the baron smiled. "It has nothing to do with what happened between you two; he caught a fever a few months ago and never recovered."

"And since then, she has been here every day; she could not even wait a year of mourning," Mary said.

"The usual rules do not cause Constance any concern," Hamish said.

"She is one who is determined, that is for sure," the baron said diplomatically.

"She comes in here unannounced as if she owns the place, and it should not be allowed," Mary continued to mutter.

"Constance gets whatever she wants. Simon found that out to his cost; it was because of some idiot idea she had that he caught the fever in the first place," Hamish said, ignoring the looks his mother was sending him.

"I used to think she was the sweetest thing. Clearly that changed when I found out she had married Simon, but still, you are describing someone I do not recognise," James said, unable to believe what he was hearing. He could not accept that Constance had changed so much if his family's descriptions of her were correct. Aside from the betrayal, his memories of her were so different.

"Pah! She is wicked and calculating," Mary said.

"That is enough, young lady! I will not have you speak of Constance like that. We are making the best of an unusual connection with her, but you cannot blame her for coming to us when she is struggling with being a widow. She had been so used to having the freedom to visit whenever she liked. Friends rally round when others are in trouble," her mother scolded.

"She is no friend of mine! How can you be so blind where she is concerned?" Mary asked, seeming to be genuinely confused at her mother's behaviour.

"I like to give people the benefit of the doubt," Lady Kirkbride replied stiffly. "Now enough of this, we have James home, and nothing is going to spoil it."

There was a sound from the doorway, and all occupants of the room turned to see who was entering.

"Hello, James."

"Hello, Constance."

“See, I was right. She thinks she owns this house,” Mary muttered to no one in particular.

Chapter 3

"I can't thank you enough for accompanying me," Alice said for the tenth time that day. "It really means a lot."

"Alice, calm down. We are nearly at the inn, not at his home." Serena smiled at her friend.

"I am sorry, I just keep thinking I am on a fool's errand."

"I wish you had decided that *before* we travelled halfway across the country."

"Ben! How can you be so brutish?"

Alice smiled. "I owe you a great debt, Ben, in accompanying us. Archie insisted that his meetings with the publishers could not be rearranged," she said of her brother.

"It is so exciting that your book will be finally in print," Serena said.

"Let us not run away with ourselves; they could say that it is not fit for public consumption," Alice cautioned.

"I do not believe that for a moment," Serena huffed.

"Can we go back to the part where I was being thanked?" Ben interrupted. "I hope when you are a rich and famous author, you will remember what I did for you."

"Oh, pfft!" Serena scoffed. "This can be practice for when you escort me across Europe."

"If I thought that you were in the slightest bit serious about travelling, I would be arguing that my need to be in London was no greater than yours. But you have been talking about the trip for so long, Serena, I am fully convinced you have absolutely no intention of undertaking the journey at all," Ben said.

Serena glared at her cousin but remained silent. Alice suspected that Ben was closer to the truth than Serena would like to admit.

As much as Alice appreciated the banter between the two cousins, it was not long before the reality of her own situation caused the smile to slip from her face. The closer she got to her destination, the more she saw the flaws in her plan. She had promised that she would wait until he had sorted out his past, but what if he could not? Her reputation would be ruined if it was known that she had followed a man into Scotland. After all, she was not writing one of her novels now, and the *ton* were not as forgiving as she could make her fictional characters. Stifling a snort, she concentrated on looking out of the window to try to hide her thoughts from Serena. Reputation? She was a bluestocking, hardly the type of person to be held up as a paragon of the season.

It did not alter the fact that she had embarked on the journey without considering the consequences. What had she been thinking? Had she been thinking? If he had felt the same way she felt about him, he would not have needed to leave. It was sobering that for the first time in her six and twenty years, she had fallen in love with someone, and he had travelled hundreds of miles away because he could not commit to her.

“Stop it,” Serena said to Alice, but glancing at her cousin, who had fallen asleep and was snoring gently.

“I do not know what you mean,” Alice responded.

“You are overthinking everything. This is the right thing to do. He cares about you deeply and will already have realised that he is missing you terribly.”

“As you have never met the oaf, you are really in for a shock when you do,” Alice said with a smile. “He is not the romantic hero I would wish him to be. I doubt he knows the meaning of romance.”

“If that is the case, it is up to you to teach him the art of being the perfect hero.”

“I am sorry to have embroiled you in this madcap scheme of chasing halfway across the country when I should be accompanying my brother in visiting publishers. It would be too much to turn around and go back, but would you mind if we just treat it as a holiday and return home in a few days?” Alice appealed to her friend, cheeks burning.

“You will not seek him out?” Serena asked incredulously.

“No. It would be wrong of me to appear so desperate and to put him under pressure to feel things he does not. We kissed, and I ran away with the idea that it meant the world to him; I was mistaken." She chose to ignore the words they had spoken, putting them down to the heat of the moment.

Serena took hold of Alice's hands and squeezed them. "I think you are doing yourself a disservice, but we shall do whatever you wish."

"You do not mind a wasted journey?" a relieved Alice asked.

"No. It has been an adventure in itself, and we are visiting a part of the country neither of us has ever seen before. Let us take some long walks and enjoy the countryside, and then we can return."

"I will not change my mind about seeing him," Alice cautioned, knowing her friend would try to persuade her to seek out Captain Avril.

"As you wish, I would just like a few days before we travel again," Serena assured her. "Ben is correct about one thing, travelling long distances can be tedious. I need to plan my journey abroad carefully."

"Are you really going to go?"

"Yes, at some point, but I admit to being daunted."

"Why go if you feel that way? No one is forcing you to embark on such a big adventure."

It was Serena's turn to sigh and look out the window for a few moments before turning back to Alice. "Does it make sense to want to do something extraordinary? That we are condemned to a life of being a spinster, a bluestocking spinster no less, and I want to show the *ton* that there can be fire and adventure inside us."

"You should be doing it for yourself, no one else," Alice said gently.

"I know, and I am, truly I am, but I cannot be remembered purely for how good my embroidery is."

Alice smiled. "It is very good, though."

"Wretch!" Serena laughed, breaking the seriousness of their conversation.

Ben snorted on a snore and opened his eyes. "Are we there yet?"

"Almost, I think," Alice replied, feeling calmer than she had since setting out on the journey.

"Thank goodness for that," Ben mumbled before falling back asleep.

***

The inn in Grantown-on-Spey was a large stone building around fifty years old. It was busy enough, and the village they had ridden through promised enough shops and surrounding countryside to entertain them for a few days. That Alice had looked at the men on the drive through the bustling village in vain for the face she longed but equally dreaded to see did not dampen her pleasure at seeing such a pretty place.

It was a planned village, with a large open square, surrounded by buildings made of the same grey stone as the inn. It seemed to contain every shop anyone could wish for, and when they alighted in the courtyard, Serena turned to Alice, a smile in place.

"This is a very pretty place, if a little chilly," she said.

"We are in the deep, dark north now; the sun never appears," Ben whispered to his cousin.

Rolling her eyes at him, she followed him into the inn and, once settled, the two women went out to explore the area while Ben remained in one of the public rooms.

"He does think we are stupid," Serena grumbled as they walked into the chilly afternoon air. "Claiming that he wanted to find out everything he could about Captain Avril's family, pah! He wants to know where the nearest gaming hell is if I know anything about my cousin."

Alice smiled. "He is a good cousin and friend, and let us hope he does find some entertainment, or he will be wishing us to return home immediately."

"When are you going to tell him that you aren't going to seek out Captain Avril after all?"

"I was hoping you would," Alice said with a grimace.

Serena laughed. "Coward!"

"Most definitely. I know how my brother would react in the same situation."

"It is as well you are such a good friend, although this will cost you a lot in bonbons," Serena warned.

"I will give you as many as you wish; even if you become sick of them, I will continue to buy them."

"I would never do that, so I hope your pockets are deep, for I am sure there is a shop here which must sell them."

"Lead on," Alice said. For the first time since arriving, she relaxed into the fact that she could treat this journey as a short holiday and nothing more. Her decision to follow James had come from the desperation which had hit her when she had told him to go and sort out his feelings for Constance. She had not wanted him to go but knew that he had to put his past to rest before they could have a future.

She should have done what she said and waited for him instead of travelling for days like some foolish heroine in one of her stories. She was a romantic, but she had been ridiculous in this instance. If her heart argued against her, she pushed the feelings aside and continued with Serena, determined that she had made the right decision to have a few days' break from travelling and then return home, with James being none the wiser of her foolhardy actions.

Chapter 4

James and Constance stared at each other. To James, Constance still looked the same, with auburn hair and blue eyes in a round face; she was tall and willowy and looked completely at home in his ancestral home.

"You came home. I knew you would," Constance said, her hand fluttering to her heart. "You responded when I needed you most."

"I came because it was time to return," James said, his tone gruff, his usual frown in place.

"But my letter must have had some impact. What I said was not written lightly," Constance said, taking a tentative step towards him.

"I burned it before reading it. I have no idea what you put," James responded.

"Oh." For the first time since she had entered, she seemed a little less sure of herself.

"This is proving even more interesting than I expected," Hamish said, exaggeratedly looking between the pair. "What did you write, Constance? I would certainly like to know, though my brother clearly could not give a fig."

Constance narrowed her eyes at Hamish. "It has nothing to do with you. It was unfinished business between your brother and I."

"There is no unfinished business," James said.

"But since Simon has gone…"

"I am sorry he died," James interrupted. "I will try to remember him for the good times we had as boys, but it is difficult."

"We never meant to hurt you."

"Having a child and marrying my best friend when you were betrothed to me was not something I was going to be happy about, was it? You could not think that I would be anything but upset, or you were both fooling yourselves or just did not know me at all."

"We were not officially betrothed. Only our families knew, and we had not announced it publicly," Constance argued.

"I had asked you to marry me, and I am a man who does not commit lightly."

"You were away so long you could have changed your mind, and I would have been cast aside."

"If you thought I could do that, you certainly know nothing about me, and you seemed happy enough to wait when replying to my letters," James said, watching emotions flit across Constance's face. He recognised some of them, mainly the petulant pout she had when a situation was not going to her liking.

"It was a hard time for me, wondering if you were dead or alive." Constance continued to play the wounded party. "I do not think you have ever appreciated what I suffered while you were away."

"And there I was having a delightful time in battle after battle, not knowing that you had a child with Simon of all people," he responded sarcastically.

"Are you telling me that you were faithful the whole time you were away?" Constance demanded.

"Of course I was. I had committed to you," James said. "I could ask how soon after I left you got together with Simon, but I do not want to know any of it. Excuse me, already I have heard too much." He walked out of the door, moving awkwardly, so he did not have to brush past Constance. She looked as if to try to stop him but changed her mind and turned back to the room with flushed cheeks.

"I am presuming that wasn't the greeting you expected to receive from my brother?" Hamish asked, clearly amused.

"Everything will be well. I will speak to him in private," Constance said. "Lady Kirkbride, please could I borrow the embroidery pattern you showed me last week? I want to make a handkerchief in the same style for my mother's birthday."

"Of course, come with me. I put it in the library after we spoke," Lady Kirkbride said, rising and glaring at her son before leaving the room.

"Hamish, you need to tread carefully; it was clear that your brother is still affected by Constance," Baron Kirkbride cautioned.

"More fool him," Mary muttered.

"For once, little sister, we are in complete agreement." Hamish smiled at her. "What he saw in her to start with, I will never know, and why Mother insists on being civil to the chit is beyond comprehension after the trick she pulled on James."

"Your mother is life-long friends with Constance's mother, as you are well aware. She wants to keep the peace between the families, and if that involves Constance feeling comfortable enough to visit, so be it. I admit, I have sometimes wondered how she can be so openly indulgent, but I am not about to question it."

"She doesn't just visit, though, does she? She walks around as if she owns the place. I would watch out, Hamish, for I think she might be considering becoming the lady of the manor when you inherit," Mary said.

Hamish laughed but then became thoughtful. "Hmm, you could have a point there, little sister. I refuse to be the one she settles on if James does not come up to scratch. If she thinks she can set her cap at me, she is sadly mistaken, that I can guarantee."

"No plotting and planning her downfall," the baron warned. "I do not want your brother half-killing you like he did with Simon. If he chooses Constance now that she is free, we accept it."

"If he is so foolish, perhaps we could claim that he is insane and prevent Constance from getting her way," Hamish mused, a glint in his eyes.

***

James walked through the woodland that he knew so well. He and Simon had explored every inch of the area when they were boys, making hiding places, climbing, fishing, and swimming.

"Why did you do it, Simon?" he muttered, roughly pushing through some of the deeper undergrowth. "I thought I could trust you with my life, and you betrayed me in the worst possible way."

Stomping over the land for more than two hours, he eventually returned to the entrance of the woodland. Surprised to see his father sitting on a fallen log, clearly waiting for him, he slowed his pace as he neared him.

Baron Kirkbride smiled at his son as he approached. "Have a sit-down. It has been a hard day for you."

"Aye, it has been a challenge, but eye-opening too, which was unexpected."

"You have only been back a day, and already you are sounding like Hamish."

"That fop? If I remind you of him, there really is no hope for me!"

The baron smiled at the response; there had always been a healthy rivalry between the brothers. "It is good to have you back, but I feel you aren't really here. In body maybe, but not in spirit."

"I do not understand your meaning." But the shuffle of discomfort as he sat on the log next to his father gave away some of his inner turmoil.

"You are no longer the man who fell in love with Constance, which is no surprise, for you were but a boy when you left."

"If I was, the wars soon woke me up to a brutal reality. I certainly was not a boy when I returned."

"I can only imagine the sights you have seen, and I am sorry for that. I only hope that you do not still suffer as a result of defending your country."

"There are the occasional nightmares," James admitted. "But as my men often said, not a lot could make me falter."

"Apart from when you set eyes on Constance again."

"What? Her arrival took me by surprise, that is all! Any feelings I had for her, well, those are in the past."

"This might sound as if I did not wish for your return, for I did, but why have you returned if the business with Constance is done with? She told us she had sent a letter to that soldier's sanctuary, but I do not think any of us believed a letter from her would bring you back, even with it containing the news about Simon's death."

"It would not have done," James said. "I have no idea what she wrote as I was speaking the truth when I said the moment I recognised her handwriting, I threw the letter in the fire."

"What changed your mind about returning then?"

"A blasted termagant of a pixie!" he growled out.

"And what did this pixie say to make you change your mind?" Baron Kirkbride asked, looking with renewed interest at his son.

"That I was stuck in the past, and she was not about to be second best. She cursed me to the devil and told me to get myself sorted out," James explained with a whoosh of breath.

"Sounds like wise words to me."

"She is too clever for her own good; she's certainly too clever for me."

"Sounds like the type of woman who would keep you on your toes and be the making of you."

James stood up and started to pace the entrance to the woodland. A few times he glanced at the opening as if weighing up whether or not to go back into the shaded area and try to clear his mind once more. The baron did not interrupt his son's obvious struggle, just took out a cigarillo and lit it as James continued to pace.

Eventually, James turned to his father. "How can I risk being betrayed again? How does everyone who commits to another not drive themselves insane, waiting to be let down?"

Blowing out a cloud of smoke, the baron looked at his son with sympathy. "You chose a flighty girl when you were very young. Yes, she was pretty, but she never had the character to match. She might have remained faithful to you if you had not been separated, but we will never know how a marriage to you would have turned out. One thing I have always known about Constance is that she is rarely satisfied with her lot and that never changed, even when she was with Simon."

"I do take some of the blame for leaving."

"Do not be so willing to absolve those who betrayed you. They would not be so quick to do the same if the situation was reversed," the baron cautioned. "As for why we risk our hearts in the first place, we do not think that anything untoward will happen, for if we did, no one would ever marry. Usually, falling in love is not a decision we consider with a cool head, for when you meet the right person, you cannot imagine life without them, and all reason is lost."

"I cannot live thinking that one day I will be betrayed again. It would be best to remain alone than to be forced to go through the pain; it was worse than going into battle."

"Then you will never be happy, and as your pixie says, always stuck in the past," the baron said, standing. "One thing, James. I understand some of why your mother wants to keep the peace between Constance's family and ours, but I have yet to find out what Constance is about. Her reasoning for being on such familiar terms is not as clear nor as selflessly motivated as your mother's reasoning is."

"You think she has me in her sights now Simon has gone?"

"Possibly. Or it could be as Mary said, and she has set her cap at Hamish in case her letter did not find you."

If the baron thought that James would be angered at his words, he did not expect the bark of laughter James let out. "Hamish? Leg-shackled to Constance? Nay, Da, he will marry some society miss with a fortune; he is too ambitious to end up with someone like Constance."

"Interesting that you think she was good enough for you but not your brother."

"I am the second son; there isn't the same pressure on me to marry well."

"I wonder if I had uttered the same words when you were together, whether you would have had the same response. And just so you know, I would like to see all my children marry well, whether they are first, second, third son, or daughter. Do not underestimate how much happiness you would be throwing away by refusing to marry the right person. Now if you would excuse me, son, I want to catch up to the bailiff, and I can see him in the top field."

James watched his father walk across the land, frown firmly in place. Would he have reacted differently as his father had suggested if they had had the same conversation before he left for war? He had thought there was no one else like Constance, but seeing her now, it was different. Yes, she was still attractive, very attractive, but it was almost as if he did not recognise her. He had expected to feel some connection to her, especially after finding out that she was now a widow, but there had been nothing. No recognition of his earlier feelings, no longing to take her into his arms and all would be well, just confusion. It was a little strange and even more unsettled his thoughts.

All that had happened was that he compared her to Alice, and Constance could not compare in a favourable way. He understood why Mary was frustrated with Constance; it was very forward of her to come and go in their family home, no matter how much his mother wanted to keep the peace. Constance had enjoyed some freedom when visiting when they were together, but not to the extent that she seemed to have now. His father was correct; her behaviour did not add up.

To his cost, he had never presumed that Constance was one to plot and seek out situations that would advance her, and he saw that was a major oversight on his part. Not for the first time, he wondered how he had got it so wrong with the two people he had cared most about.

One thing was becoming apparent to him, the person he missed the most was Simon. Strange, when it should be Constance who had promised to be his. But his return home had proved one thing to him, he was not as stuck in the past as he had thought.

Smiling for what felt like the first time since he had arrived home, he stood and turned towards the town. He would visit Simon's grave and make peace with his friend in the only way he could. Enough time had been wasted; it was time to look to the future.

Chapter 5

Alice and Serena set out across the footpaths which covered the area. It was their third day at the inn, and they had settled into a routine of exploring as much as they could. This morning they had walked along the River Spey before turning away from the water and heading over the fields.

"This is beautiful. I think my next book will be set in the Highlands; it would be perfect for a gothic romance," Alice said as they walked, not another person in sight.

"With a handsome Highlander at the centre?" Serena teased.

"Maybe," Alice responded with a sideways glance at her friend, a laugh in her voice. "On the other hand, I might have to make him the dastardly villain and kill him off."

"Alice!" Serena exclaimed. "Remind me to never upset you. Here am I thinking you are the quietest member of the Bluestocking Club; it seems I have underestimated you."

"I am!" Alice laughed. "I put all my wickedness in my stories."

"In that case, I hope your brother secures a publisher soon, and we can read this novel. I want to see who you secretly dislike!"

Alice smiled. "I might not admit to which new release is mine."

"You couldn't do that to us! We are desperate to read your book."

"Probably not. I have enough vanity to want my friends to tell me how wonderful I am."

It was Serena's turn to laugh. "Now I know you are funning with me. You are the most modest person I know."

Alice was about to reply when she was thrown forward as she took a step. Landing on the rough path they had been walking along, she let out a cry of pain. "My ankle!" she moaned, feeling nauseous as the searing pain shot up through her leg.

"Let me help," Serena said, immediately crouching and trying to lift Alice.

"Ow! Ow! Ow!" Alice exclaimed at every movement she was forced to make as Serena tried to help her up.

"I am sorry," Serena responded, trying to be gentle.

"It's not your fault, oh! Ouch! Oh dear, I feel quite ill."

Serena eventually managed to help Alice to sit up rather than remain face first in the dirt, but she had paled further once in the new position and looked to be about to faint.

"Blasted rabbits!" Alice moaned, her head hanging, her breathing shallow.

"We can stay here until the pain passes, and then we can take it very slowly back to the inn," Serena soothed. "There is no need to move immediately."

"The way I am feeling now, I think I want to remain here all night," Alice groaned, swallowing convulsively.

"Let me take a look," Serena said, moving Alice's skirts so she could see. The boot was twisted at a funny angle, which made Serena wince.

"Oh! Please do not touch it! It is too painful."

"I will not touch it again; best to leave it until we can get help."

"Is it bad?" Alice asked through gritted teeth.

"I think it is broken. We will not be hobbling back to the inn; there is too much of a risk of causing more damage. I need to get help."

"I am sorry for being a goose," Alice groaned. "You should not be wandering through the countryside alone to find someone to assist me. Your cousin will not be happy."

"Then he should have accompanied us instead of deserting us for a cock fight," Serena said. "I will be as quick as I can."

"Do not hurry. I do not want you falling too, or we will be in a real fix."

"Are you comfortable?" Serena asked. "Can I help you to sit in any way that will cause you the least discomfort, for we have been walking for some time. It might take me a while to find someone."

“I will be fine like this unless you have a cushion about your person, of course,” Alice said with a flicker of a smile. “The ground is a trifle hard, but at least I am sat up. There is little dignity in being sprawled across the ground.”

Serena gave her friend a quick embrace before standing, brushing her dress down as best she could and looking back the way they had come. “I will be as quick as I can.”

Alice watched her friend disappear and tried to get more comfortable herself. All that happened was that her foot moved, and the nausea and faintness washed over her again. “Oh blast it, Alice, only you could spoil an adventure by falling down a rabbit hole,” she muttered to herself. “I suppose it serves me right for trying to act the heroine and chase the hero. One would think that, by now, I would have accepted being a spinster.”

Continuing to curse and chide herself, she began to feel cool as a chill from the ground seeped through her skirts, and shivering, she wondered how long she would be stuck in the undignified position. Even a thick woollen dress was no match for the cold earth. Rubbing her arms to try and generate some heat, she continued to mutter to herself. “It will serve you right if you die of a chill, and then you will definitely be the heroine of a gothic novel, and he will not even know you have been in the area. I never realised what a pathetic creature I could be.”

With much relief and far sooner than she had expected, she saw Serena walking towards her, a gentleman in company with her. Alice tried to make herself look presentable, which, as she was almost prone on the ground, was not an easy task. She could tell whoever he was that he was a gentleman with his fine clothes and assured gait, which somehow made her feel even more foolish.

Serena approached Alice with a smile on her face; she had been chattering as she walked, clearly at ease with the stranger. As they got closer, the man looked very distinguished, with grey hair and vivid green eyes, definitely not the farm hand she had expected Serena to return with.

He smiled down at Alice when he reached her. "Och, our wildlife has attacked you, has it?"

"It is embarrassing that I was felled by the home of a fluffy rabbit. It would have done my reputation far more good to have been attacked by something vicious," Alice said.

"If you had, I might have fainted at the sight of blood," he chuckled at her.

"Alice, this is Baron Kirkbride. He was with his bailiff when I came across them," Serena explained. "My lord, this is my dear friend, Miss Alice Boyd."

"It is a pleasure to make your acquaintance, Miss Boyd. I am only sorry that it is not under more pleasant circumstances."

"I am sorry to have caused you any trouble, my lord," Alice said, feeling even worse that he had been inconvenienced.

"Not at all. I have sent my bailiff for a cart of some sort to convey you to my home, but would you mind if I carried you to the farm track? He will not be able to navigate along this path."

"If you could lend me your arm, I could hop," Alice said.

"From what your friend has told me of your injury, if it touches the ground, we will have you fading away in a dead faint. A possible broken ankle is not to be taken lightly. We need to get you some medical help and soon."

"Bother!" Alice said. "I am so sorry. I do not do this, I promise you."

"Do what?" Baron Kirkbride asked with some amusement.

"Cause a fuss. I blend into the background and just watch."

"And then she writes about the foibles of others to be published and make us mortified when we recognise ourselves in one of her novels," Serena laughed.

A slight frown crossed Baron Kirkbride's face before he smiled once more. Alice took the change in his demeanour as a dislike of her being a writer, which was no surprise. Most thought it a poor profession, especially for a young lady.

"I can assure you, there is no need to apologise. You are more than welcome to stay at my home until you have recovered fully, however long that takes."

"Oh no! We are most comfortable at the inn," Alice said quickly.

The baron looked at Serena. "You and your cousin are more than welcome to join Miss Boyd. I assure you she will be far more comfortable with my family than in the inn. Now it is time to move, Miss Boyd?" He asked permission to pick Alice up, and reluctantly she nodded her approval. With almost no effort, he lifted her into his arms and started walking back the way he had come, with Serena following.

***

Alice spent most of the journey apologising over and over until the baron turned to Serena with a smile. "Is she always so apologetic?"

"She is too nice for her own good," Serena replied.

"I was beginning to get that impression."

"I am not so meek as you describe," Alice said with a huff.

"That is good news indeed," the Baron said enigmatically.

Once on the cart, Alice was made as comfortable as possible, and as they travelled, the baron explained about the area, trying to distract Alice from her discomfort until they reached the lodge house of his home. Waving at the gatekeeper, they trundled through the gates and onto the drive which was flanked on either side by trees.

"This is a beautiful place," Alice said.

"Thank you. I hope to see it one day in one of your novels," the baron said.

"I am not published and probably never will be."

"You sound like my son. He writes poetry and revels in being a troubled soul. I should warn you that the moment he realises you are a writer, he will bombard you with questions."

Alice smiled. "I will have little that is of use to tell him, but it will be nice to be able to speak to a fellow writer. He will understand the torture which is real when the page remains blank."

"Now here was I thinking that you would never be short of inspiration."

Alice looked away for a moment. "When I am content, I find the words flow," she said quietly.

"In that case, I hope to provide you with a place of sanctuary."

Arriving at the large stone house, Alice was lifted from the cart by the baron, which made her cheeks flush, especially when the door was opened and a bustle of activity ensued.

The doctor had already been sent for by the bailiff when he had collected the cart from the nearest farm, and he arrived moments after Alice was settled in a guest chamber. She was still constantly apologising for the trouble she was causing.

"Now we shall have no more," Lady Kirkbride said. "As my husband said, you are more than welcome here for as long as is needed. You all are," she said to

Serena. "If you would like to send a note to your cousin while the doctor is examining Miss Boyd, we can have you all settled by nightfall."

"Thank you," Serena said, following Lady Kirkbride out of the room.

The doctor took his time examining Alice's foot. It was a trial when he had to cut the boot off, and Alice reacted by casting up her accounts, which mortified her, but the doctor calmly tended her until the boot could be removed. Her foot was strapped in place, and after giving her some laudanum, he stepped back, putting his frock coat on.

"You are young and healthy. With rest and the acceptance that you cannot go running around the countryside for some time, you should fully recover. I do not think it is broken, but it is one of the worst sprains I have ever seen. Try and walk on it too early and you could end up with a limp," the doctor instructed.

"I will not try to move, but when will I be able to travel? We were only supposed to be in the area for a few days," Alice said, already feeling the numbing effects of the medicine.

"There is no need to worry about that at the moment," Lady Kirkbride said as she came into the room. "I have told Miss Formby there is no hurry; we are more than happy to have company."

"You are very kind," Alice said.

"Nonsense, we are doing what anyone would do."

Alice's eyes were closing when she heard the bang of the door slamming against the wall; it had been opened with such force. She looked towards the door to see Captain Avril, seeming to fill the doorway, hands on hips, staring at her.

"Ali— Miss Boyd, what the devil are you doing in my house and what have you done to yourself?" he demanded, looking between the three occupants of the room.

"James! Manners!" Lady Kirkbride scolded.

"Oh blast, this cannot be your home. I cannot be that unlucky," Alice said, her words slurring with the effort to remain awake.

"It has been my family home for the last three generations."

"Just when I had decided that I was not going to see you again, you have to appear, looking as magnificent as always, whilst I look a sight. What an awkward beast you are, Captain Avril," Alice said, closing her eyes and starting to gently snore.

Chapter 6

"He was absolutely dumbstruck," Lady Kirkbride said to her husband after explaining what had passed in the bedchamber.

"Ah, so she is the one who has turned his world upside down. I thought it was too much of a coincidence for it not to be the lass who he is pining over," Baron Kirkbride said with a smile.

"She must have followed him here. That is most forward behaviour to show; it is shocking that a young lady would do something so brazen."

"From the little James has said, she is very much a lady but knows our son well. She is the one who sent him home to sort himself out."

"Oh. How strange. She must have suspected he may still have feelings for Constance."

"I think she realised that he was still in love with the memory of Constance rather than the reality. He still blames himself for leaving."

"He does not!" Lady Kirkbride stiffened with indignation. "He was the one putting his life at risk, and she betrayed him in the worst possible way."

"They both did," Baron Kirkbride reminded his wife.

She sighed. "I never thought Simon would hurt James."

"No, nor I, but I feel there is a lot we do not know about what went on between Simon and Constance. Now Simon has passed, we will probably never know the truth."

"And now there is a chance that James will rekindle whatever he had with Constance."

"Not if we do something instead of sitting back and watching a disaster unfold as we did last time."

"What are you planning?" his wife asked suspiciously.

"Nothing more than allowing James and Miss Boyd to spend as much time together as they can. Constance is not the only one who can plan and plot."

"He was very upset that she was injured, I do not think he could believe she had followed him, but I saw no condemnation in his words or look. In fact, I think he was impressed by her actions," Lady Kirkbride acknowledged.

"Exactly. And an invalid needs entertaining, and if her friend is busy with Mary, well, all the more reason that James should be in her company. After all, he knows her better than the rest of us."

"I never knew you were so devious."

"Only when it is of benefit to my family," Baron Kirkbride said, leaning across to kiss his wife. "Other than that, I am but a simple soul."

"Pfft," Lady Kirkbride responded, but any other comments were forgotten as her husband deepened his kiss.

***

Alice's eyes fluttered open, immediately noticing that it was dark outside and a fire was blazing in the grate. Without turning her head, she knew who sat next to the bed.

"This was not how I planned things," she croaked, licking her dry lips.

"I seem to be spending most of my time recently sitting by the side of a sick bed," James said, moving to offer Alice a glass of water.

"I never had you down as one for the dramatics," she said after he had lifted her and she had taken a grateful sip.

"And I did not expect you to chase across country after me."

"That was a mistake," Alice said, cheeks burning.

"Was it?" James was watching her intently, his expression betraying none of what he felt.

"Of course it was! I had sent you on your way and then realised you were nodcock enough to make a cake of yourself, so I decided I needed to follow you. By the time I reached Scotland, I realised my idea was foolish in the extreme. There is no need to condemn me for my hoydenish behaviour; I have cursed myself to the devil."

"Ah, you must be the young lady who is the fearless adventurer," Hamish drawled from the open doorway.

"I am the person who cannot walk in a straight line without falling over like some feeble chit," Alice responded.

"I find it can be a difficult task, especially when one is foxed, not that I am suggesting you were of course. Please allow me to introduce myself, the Honourable Hamish Avril at your service, madam. Elder brother of the war hero that is my brother," he said, bowing over Alice's hand and sending a disparaging look towards James.

"You forgot rake and wastrel in your introduction," James said.

"I would never reveal your biggest faults to such a delicate young lady."

Alice could not help the laugh escaping at the glare James sent his brother. "Be careful, sir. He does not take criticism well."

"Oh, I know, but between us, we should be able to make him fairly civilised once he stops wearing that kilt like it is some token or something. I am sure I can smell it the moment I walk into the house."

"It is in pristine condition!" James responded. "It is my heritage."

"So is running around and fighting the English, but we have stopped doing that. You only need to wear the blasted thing on formal occasions. Why do you have to always have your knees on show?"

"Though they are fine knees," Alice said, laughing but blushing at her audacity.

"I assure you, mine are far superior for not being constantly bare to the elements," Hamish said.

"I like your brother," Alice said to James.

"Everyone does until they find out his true character."

"I am wounded," Hamish said, hand on heart.

"I see dramatics run in your family," Alice said to James, at which Hamish barked with laughter.

"Miss Boyd, you are a delight, but I must warn you, our youngest brother is the most dramatic of us all."

"Is he the writer of the family?"

"Yes, and is itching to come and annoy you; thankfully, Mother has forbidden it. We do not wish you to throw yourself out of the window in an effort to escape Drew."

"I do not mind speaking to him," Alice said.

"I would build your strength up first," James said. "I have only been back a short time, but I quickly came to realise that Drew can be quite intense."

"Another trait which runs in the family," Alice muttered but smiled at Hamish's chuckle.

"James, she is a delight. I congratulate you on finding a diamond. Miss Boyd, I look forward to getting to know you better." With a flourishing bow, Hamish left the room, leaving Alice and James both silent.

"I am sorry," Alice eventually said.

"What for?"

"Being a fool. I will leave the moment I am able."

James stood and walked to the window, closing the heavy drapes. "What if I would like you to stay?"

Alice's heart lifted at his words, but she knew she had not been fair in chasing him across country. "Then I would mix up your thoughts, and you would not be able to make a clear decision about your future."

"All I have thought about is you from the moment I left," James said.

"That is a good start. Dare I be vain enough to say that I am happy to hear that you missed me?" Alice asked coyly.

James flashed one of his rare smiles at her. "Lassie, I was as tormented as Drew claims to be when I travelled here. Every mile I wanted to demand the stage be turned around to travel back to you."

Holding out her hand to bring him back, Alice squeezed his fingers when he crossed to her. "I am spoiled for anyone else since the moment I saw you, but I need you to make a decision about your past. I have been foolish by chasing you and unfair, I know that, but I stand by what I said. I cannot be second best."

"You would never be that. Not to me."

"Then Constance stirs nothing within you?" she asked hopefully.

James's face clouded, destroying the ray of hope Alice had seen. "She stirs something, but I do not know what it is yet. I cannae work it out, it is confusing me, and I wish I could clear my mind, for it is driving me half insane."

"Then I would ask you leave me be and go and find out why she still affects you. If you still care for her, then that is the end of it," Alice said sharply.

"Lassie, I do not say the words to upset you," James said, stroking her cheek. "That is the last thing I want."

"I know, but it does hurt and always will until you make a decision," Alice said, cupping his hand and crushing it to her cheek as if she wanted never to let go of him. "Go now, for this is prolonging the torture."

"I am sorry."

"As am I."

***

Ben and Hamish were to find kindred spirits when they met, and both were away over the coming days at some place which promised a good time. Serena and Mary spent their time with Lady Kirkbride or with Alice, especially when Drew had spent as much of the day with Alice as he could.

On the fourth day, Alice had begged to be carried downstairs, and after a lot of persuasion, James had agreed, carrying her down and laying her on a sofa in the drawing room.

"I want no attempts at moving, or you will be sent back to bed," James said, having reluctantly let go of her. Having Alice's arms around his neck and her head tucked into his shoulder had stirred feelings within him that he wanted to continue. Only because the other women were already in the room did he restrain from kissing Alice as he placed her down.

"Yes, Captain," Alice said.

"Do not try and convince my family that you are meek. I have told them exactly what you are like."

"That is something you would do," Alice cursed him. "I am still trying to convince them that I am of good character."

James's lips quirked. "Do not try to do the impossible."

"Brute."

"You would not have me any other way."

"Oh what a cosy scene you all portray," Constance's voice came from the doorway. "Am I interrupting something?"

"I knew she would be somewhere around," Mary muttered to Serena.

"Of course not," Lady Kirkbride said. "Come in and meet our guests."

"I have stayed away for the last few days because Mother has not been well," Constance explained, walking into the room and clearly assessing the strangers.

"Is she improved?" Lady Kirkbride asked.

"She is, thank you."

Lady Kirkbride conducted the introductions, and Constance smiled and said her hellos, but there was ice underneath her greeting. She was watching James and taking in the others at the same time.

When she was seated, she folded her hands on her lap. "I was hoping that James would help me with Cameron," she said.

"And why would I do that?" James demanded.

"Because Simon is dead, and you were his best friend."

"I was, but that was before he acted the cad." James could see that Constance was unhappy with his constant referral to her betrayal, but he did not see why he should let her forget it, especially as he was wary of her current motivations.

"One day, James, we will have a conversation about the reality of what happened before you left. You have never asked about my side of the story," Constance snapped, once more the petulant look firmly in place.

"Perhaps I do not wish to know," James said and walked out of the room with only a pained glance at Alice.

"You seem to have the knack of being able to send my brother out of rooms in the shortest time. You had best teach me how you do it so I can be forearmed if I receive any unwanted attention from a beau," Mary said.

"With your sharp retorts, I would presume you are to be a spinster, so you will have nothing to worry about," Constance responded.

"Constance! You forget yourself!" Lady Kirkbride reprimanded her visitor.

Constance flushed and lowered her head. "I apologise, but she always tries to make me feel unwelcome. I hear all her comments, however quietly muttered. I am sure she says them loud enough to ensure I hear them and feel uncomfortable." When she looked up, there were tears in her eyes, and she sent a look of anguish to Lady Kirkbride.

"Two wrongs do not make a right, you are old enough to realise that, and I would expect better behaviour from you, especially towards one of my family," Lady Kirkbride said. "Mary, I expect you to treat our guests appropriately. It is not fair to torment Constance as you do. You are not a child."

"I will be better, Ma. But can I point out that guests do not tend to walk in and out at will? It is quite perturbing how she suddenly appears. Who knows what she could overhear? We should not need to be circumspect in our own house."

"That be as it may, Constance deserves the courtesy that everyone else does."

"Yes, Ma."

"Good. Now please order some fresh refreshments, and we can have a civilised conversation."

Mary shot a look at Drew, who had remained silent in the corner as she got up to ring the servant's bell. It was clear to anyone who saw the exchange that brother and sister would reluctantly tolerate Constance to pacify their mother.

Chapter 7

James had brought out an invalid chair to allow Alice to get some fresh air. Alice had complained at the need to be pushed around, but she was too keen to be out of doors not to accept the help.

"It is a good thing you are a giant, or you would be in bed with exhaustion for the next week after pushing this chair for any length of time."

"Ah, you are nothing but a feather, but it is good to know that you have noticed how strong I am." James smiled down at her.

"As I have said before, one would have to be blind to not realise the size of you means you are a big oaf," Alice retorted, but there was a smile on her lips.

"Aye, but I am your big oaf, lassie."

Alice hoped he was speaking the truth but refused to bring up Constance when they were enjoying each other's company. She had visited every morning since Alice had been brought downstairs and only left when everyone had a headache and the joy of the day had gone. Alice wondered seriously and not out of jealousy what James had seen in her because she had not the personality or attractive nature that Alice had expected.

"Drew has real talent," Alice said, changing the subject.

"I am glad. I just wish he was not quite so dramatic with his prose."

"That is because he is still young, and all boys want to be like Byron."

"More fool him," James muttered.

"Do not be like that," Alice chided. "You cannot convince me that you are not in awe of the Duke of Wellington."

"He is a war hero!" James said, defending his leader. "He did not waste the day writing nonsense that no one would see."

"I am glad to understand how you consider my occupation."

James swung the chair around to face him and bent down so he was level with Alice; the twinkle in his eyes matched the smile on her lips. "Now listen to me, lassie. I do not think anyone can put pen to paper as you can."

"Said without ever reading a word I have written," Alice responded.

"Oh, have I not? You should be more careful where you leave your pages," James said, smile broadening.

"When? Where? I never leave anything lying around." Alice looked mortified.

"You did one day at Hesketh Hall, and I could not help satisfying my curiosity. You have a fine way with words, lassie," James responded, sounding as proud as if he had written the words himself.

"Blast you to the devil. You can compliment me whilst at the same time making me mortified and embarrassed."

"I happen to like it when those cheeks are rosy, especially after I have kissed you," James said, kissing her gently on the lips.

Alice pulled away. "We should not."

"Aye, you are right, but I want to," James sighed.

"I never want to refuse anything you want," Alice said. Her voice was quiet, but her words were bold.

"Lassie, words like that make my heart sing." He knelt on the hard ground, ignoring the effect on his knees, and taking her in his arms, he kissed her as he had when she had recovered from the attack at Hesketh Hall.

Alice had wanted to be kissed from the moment she had set eyes on James, and wrapping her arms around his neck, she revelled in the feel of him, the passion he poured into every kiss and encouraged him to continue by thoroughly kissing him back.

Only separating when they were both breathless, they rested their foreheads together. "You are wicked," James said.

"With you I am."

James groaned. "I need a special licence and a clergyman."

"Only when you are fully ready," Alice cautioned. "And when you ask in a more romantic way."

"You know I am no poet or one for flowery language."

"I also know that when you wish to, you can be the most eloquent of anyone I know."

James snorted. "With speeches like that, I would have thought you had been brought up in a convent, not surrounded by intelligent women," he said of Alice's Bluestocking friends.

Alice punched him on the arm, making him chuckle. "Take me back. You do not deserve any more kisses. Not today, at least."

"In that case, I cannae wait until tomorrow. I can see our excursions outside are going to get longer and longer. Woe betide anyone who suggests they join us," James said, turning the chair around and heading back to the house.

"Oh, I think the looks you shot at everyone when you said you were taking me outside were enough to send a clear message to them all. No one dared suggest accompanying us."

"Long may it continue."

Alice leaned back in the chair while James pushed her along the pathways. He had all but proposed marriage, and although stunned at his utterances, she had managed to sound unmoved when she answered, demanding a more romantic proposal. The truth was that her heart had soared at his mention of a special licence. She had told him she could only accept him when he had made a decision. Did this mean that he had? He did not seem like one who would get carried away in the moment, but for now she would have to wait and see. And hope. She was definitely going to hope.

***

Constance smiled as she approached James. She had purposely come to visit later than she usually did with the aim of speaking to him alone. The farce had gone on long enough, and although he had become slightly more civil to her, she could see that something had developed between him and the bluestocking, and his family were encouraging the budding romance. She knew nothing of their past but still could not sit by and let whatever they had turn serious, so it was time to act. Squaring her shoulders, she braced herself for what was to come.

“Good afternoon, James. Have you already been out on your walk with Miss Boyd?”

“Yes,” James answered curtly, cursing the fact that he had set out for the stables just when Constance had arrived, thinking he had avoided her for the day.

“I notice that you always come back with a smile on your face after your walks. I remember when I could make you smile like that. You were so considerate, so loving, and you made my heart swell with happiness.”

“I do not wish to go over what happened in the past. It is done.”

“That is where you are wrong, James. We need to talk. We can do it in front of your family. I am sure you would rather not, but if it is the only way I can make you listen to what I have to say, I will do it. I will regret upsetting your mother, for she has been very good to me, but it cannot be helped," Constance said, putting her hand on James's arm to prevent him from moving away.

James shook her hand off him, put his hands on his hips and scowled at Constance. "What do you want from me? You have shown that you do not love me. You marrying someone else was a message I heard loud and clear. If you think now that Simon has gone that we can carry on like before, then you consider me a bigger fool than I look."

"I want you to take responsibility for what is yours! That is all I have ever wanted from you, but you were never around when you were needed. This time I insist you face up to your duty," Constance snapped.

"What are you talking about, woman? You have nothing that is mine," James spat. "I always tried to do what was right. Now leave me be."

"You have a son who needs a father!"

James had started to storm away from Constance, but at her words, he stopped. His shoulders heaved as he faced away from her, making Constance wonder how he was going to react. Eventually, he turned to face her, his expression furious. "You are trying to claim that I am father to your boy? I have heard all the low tricks that anyone can try. Have you no decency? Trying to convince an innocent man that he is the father of your son. You disgust me."

James saw that his words had hit home. Constance's eyes flashed. "He is yours, and Simon knew it. You always thought you had been betrayed, but it was only when I found out that I was increasing with no hope of saving my reputation that Simon stepped in to save mine and your reputations. He had done you the best service a friend could do."

"You are lying!" James roared. "We never laid together. I left you an innocent."

Constance flinched at the words and the volume of his shout but shook her head. "It happened the night before you left. You were foxed, and we went to the barn; remember you woke up there? I am trying not to be offended that you cannot remember what happened between us."

James walked a few steps away, hand pulling at his hair before looking once more at Constance. "This is not true. I have never been so out of my senses that I would take your innocence in a barn! I am not such a brute."

"Maybe not now, but you were going away, and I think the thought of what you were going to face made you act rashly. You were not cruel to me."

"This cannot be happening. Not now," James muttered to himself, cursing and walking away from Constance and then back to her. "It cannot be true."

"It is. He is just like you, tall, blonde with blue eyes," Constance said quietly. "He is a good boy."

"You have just described Simon's colouring; you know full well that we could have been brothers we were so alike. How can I believe you after all you have done?"

"I would not lie about this. I am going to tell Cameron that the father he loved was not his father and that a stranger is, in fact, related to him. Do you think I would do that just to torment you in some way? What possible gain could I get from my actions? Why would I upset my son like that? You must really think the worst of me to consider that I could hurt Cameron when he is all I have left of our time together." Constance had spoken calmly, and with her words, James seemed to deflate before her.

"What do you want me to do? I will support him obviously, but I can do no more for either of you," he said.

Walking to James, Constance touched his face. "Let this be the reason to allow us to have another chance at being together. We were both young and foolish; we are more worldly now. No one would think it strange to see us rekindle what we once shared." Leaning her head on his shoulder, she sighed. "I have missed you so much, James. I know we can be happy again; you just have to give us another chance."

James pulled away. "I love Alice," he said simply.

"I know you hold her in affection," Constance said. "But ours was a first love, the strongest kind of love. I have known you all your life. Does she know that you could never live in London, that you need the wide-open spaces of your homeland to feel whole?"

"She would move here."

"Have you asked her?"

James shook his head. "No."

"You have not planned out your future as we did?" Constance asked, her eyes sparkling. "Remember how we would sit for hours and decide how many children we would have, what our house would be like and what animals we would keep. Do not look on what Simon did as a betrayal; consider that he cared for your most precious possessions until you returned."

"You are asking me to marry you?" he asked, mind racing with disbelief.

"I am; however forward that makes me sound."

"You do not seem to have a problem with being forthright with what you want. You never seemed to be like that, not with me anyway. I am not sure I ever knew the real you," James said sarcastically.

"No. I suppose I am different to how you remember me. One could even say that it was out of necessity that I had to change, married to a man I did not want because the man I longed for had abandoned me with child and few options," Constance snapped, finally losing her temper when he had not reacted as compliantly as she had expected. "You have never had to worry, knowing that people were talking about you because you married someone new and the bairn arrived very soon after the wedding. I am still looked down on to this day, and I am sick of it."

"What are you saying?"

"If you do not do the decent thing and provide a home for Cameron and myself, I am going to tell everyone the truth about our situation. I will also let it be known that your mother and father knew and were letting me visit in order to keep me sweet and not besmirch the reputation of their hero son."

"My reputation will be able to stand it," James said with derision. "But will yours? From what you said, hardly anyone will believe your accusations."

"At this point, it does not matter." Constance shrugged. "We have little to live off and no prospects. It is irrelevant if your mother and father experience some shame for their bad behaviour having rejected their first grandson."

"You really are an unpleasant creature. I have no idea what I ever saw in you, for you are the worst woman that I know," James said.

"Do the decent thing by Cameron and myself, and I will return to the meek and pleasing woman you fell in love with."

James was silent for a long time, Constance could not work out which way he was going to respond, but finally he sighed in defeat.

"I will never love you, and I am no longer going to try and fool myself into thinking that you ever really loved me. I doubt you have ever loved anyone other than yourself. I will do as you ask, for the boy, not for you. He deserves to be recognised for who his family is and get his inheritance. But know this, madam, I will never lay with you, nor will there be anything more than civility between us and believe me, it will cost me a great deal to be civil."

Constance smiled despite his harsh words. "You are doing the right thing. Thank you on Cameron's behalf."

James shrugged. “I have little choice if I want to avoid my family being affected by this mess. One thing I would ask, you say nothing until I have spoken to Alice.”

Annoyance flitted across Constance’s face, and although she schooled her features quickly, it was not fast enough. James saw the expression and knew that although he had been manipulated and played for a fool, what he had said was true; he had little choice in the matter if he was to do the right thing. Even if he refused to marry Constance, he knew that Alice would never marry him, not when she found out that he had abandoned a pregnant woman. Alice had scruples, and she would not forgive his poor behaviour, just as he was struggling with it. Having always prided himself on being an honourable man, Constance had managed to tap into the shame he had felt at laying with her and being unable to remember it. He was disgusted with her but more so with himself. Just when he thought his happiness was secured, his own drunken actions had destroyed any chance of the contentment and love he had hoped for.

“I mean it, Constance. She hears what we are doing from me, in my own time, or nothing happens between us, son or not. I owe her that,” he said.

“I do not like it, but I suppose I can give you a few days,” Constance conceded. “But do not take me for a fool, James, or I will make sure you all pay.”

“Oh, believe me, I have no problem imagining what you would be prepared to do. Now leave my home.”

"But I have come to see your mother."

"Leave. I need time away from you, and you have no right to parade around my house."

"I will have soon," Constance said with glee. "But I will return home, this once. Goodbye, James, we are doing the right thing."

James turned away from Constance, not wishing her to see the pain in his eyes nor the tears on his cheeks when he thought of never being with Alice.

Chapter 8

Constance entered Kirkbride House two days later, a wide smile on her face. In the drawing room, she greeted Lady Kirkbride, Mary and Serena as if they were long-lost friends.

"I could not resist walking over earlier than normal, it is such a lovely day," she said.

"It is cloudy," Mary responded.

"Sometimes it is what is within us that gives us renewed excitement for the day. I have sent for Cameron, and his uncle has replied that I may go and collect him," she said to Lady Kirkbride.

"Really?" Lady Kirkbride asked. "We have not seen him for a while now; he must have grown."

"Yes, he is tall and strong, just like his father. I have decided that living with Simon's uncle is one thing, but he needs to visit his mama and keep in touch with his family around these parts."

"I did not realise you had many relatives beyond your own mother," Mary said, frown in place whenever she was forced to listen to Constance.

"There are a few," Constance responded. "Where is James?"

"Probably with Miss Boyd," Mary responded.

"I expect you are thankful that I insisted on writing to Miss Hesketh in the hope that it brought James home," Constance said to Lady Kirkbride, ignoring Mary's dig.

"I am very happy to have him home," Lady Kirkbride said, unusually wary of Constance.

"You all thought I was foolish, but it did not take him long after reading my letter to return home, where he should always be."

"He did not read your letter. You can hardly claim credit for bringing him home," Mary scoffed.

"Recognising the handwriting was enough. He has acknowledged that he knew it was from me."

"Yes, he recognised who had written it and threw it in the fire. I would not be convinced of your effect on my brother," Mary said.

"You may mock, but we have a history which goes beyond the anger and hurt that my marriage to Simon caused. A history that is too important to just be thrown away. We have come to an understanding which will benefit us all."

"I think you will find it was Miss Boyd who sent him home," Serena said. She had been quiet around Constance every time they had met, observing her, but apart from the necessary pleasantries had not entered into any conversations with her. Now though, she felt compelled to speak.

"Miss Boyd?" Constance asked, clearly surprised. "You knew James before visiting here?"

"Not I, but Miss Boyd did. She was staying at Hesketh Hall helping our friend when your letter arrived. She was the one who said Captain Avril should return home."

"Did she now?" Constance had clearly not realised there was a connection between Alice and James, and for a moment she looked troubled at the knowledge but suddenly brightened. "She followed him here!" she exclaimed with a caustic laugh.

Serena looked fit to throttle Constance but was clearly cursing herself too for the information she had given Alice's rival.

"Oh, how pitiful," Constance continued.

"I think it is romantic," Mary responded, giving her mother a look.

At that moment, Hamish opened the door to allow Ben entrance, carrying Alice, surprising the others that it was not James carrying her. But for his relations and Serena at least, they were glad James was not in the room, for Constance looked gleeful at seeing Alice.

Placing her on the sofa, Ben stood back. "I am going to the inn to collect any mail that has been sent through. I asked them to keep it to one side," he said. "Is there anything you need whilst I am out?"

"No thank you," Alice said.

"I am going to accompany him, Mother," Hamish said.

"What fight or race have you found out about today?" Mary asked her brother.

Hamish grinned at his sister. "There might be a race in Aviemore this afternoon that we could stumble across."

"Though it is in the opposite direction," Mary pointed out.

"Have to give the horses a good run," Hamish said, kissing his mother. "Here again, Constance? You really are here every day, aren't you?"

"Your mother has always been very welcoming, and I hope to repay that kindness in the future."

Shaking his head at her in bemusement, Hamish bid the room goodbye and the two men were gone. The room lapsed into silence for a few moments until Constance could contain herself no longer.

"It seems I was under the illusion that I had brought James home, but it appears his family and I have you to thank, Miss Boyd," she said, breaking the uncomfortable silence.

"Oh?" Alice responded, not willing to reveal anything to the woman she did not like and not only because of what Constance had shared with James.

"I must say following him home is very – what can I say? – adventurous, perhaps. Bold, that is it, very bold behaviour. Surprising behaviour for a gentlewoman, this kind of conduct must be tolerated in London more than it would be around these parts. Perhaps we are rustic, but we do believe that ladies should act appropriately, especially unmarried ones."

Alice flushed beet red and did not say anything. Lady Kirkbride stood and held her hand out to Constance. "Come, my dear, I will walk you out, for I have errands to run, and I wish the girls to accompany me," she said.

“I can take myself off,” Constance said. She stood, clearly pleased with the mortified look on Alice’s face.

“No, let me show you to the door,” Lady Kirkbride said firmly. Constance flashed a look of surprise at her hostess, not used to receiving anything but the most considerate indulgence. Taking a firm hold of Constance’s arm, Lady Kirkbride left the room whilst the others stared at each other.

Only when Lady Kirkbride returned alone did Mary break the silence. “Ma, she is getting worse. She is rude and offensive, and I cannot understand how you stand by and allow it. No other lady of the house would accept such behaviour under their own roof.”

“I know, her behaviour since James has returned has been appalling. I think she is threatened by Miss Boyd’s presence.”

“I am sorry, Alice,” Serena said with real remorse. “I did not realise she would act so despicably when finding out that you knew Captain Avril prior to him coming home.”

“It does not matter. She was right with one point, I followed him, and no lady of class should have done such a thing,” Alice said. She was not about to mention the conversations she had shared with James about their future. Until it was official, it was important to keep their plans to themselves.

“Anyone connected to James and seeing the way he lights up and smiles when you are around can never condemn you, my dear. He has always been one to keep his feelings close to his chest, but I do not think he can help himself where you are concerned. It has been a pleasure to see, so yes, your being here was out of the ordinary, but I am glad to see my boy happy," Lady Kirkbride said.

"And his sister is too," Mary said with a smile at Alice. "I would have hated Constance as a sister-in-law."

"Thank you both for saying that, but really, there is nothing to tell..."

"We will not push you to reveal any secrets, but just know we are happy that you are here."

"Ma! We should push her for information! The sooner this is settled to all our happiness, the better," Mary said.

They were interrupted by James, who seemed surprised and unhappy that the women were gathered. He looked at Alice with such an expression of despair that she reached out her hand to him in an unconscious gesture.

"What is it?" Alice asked.

"Nothing," he responded gruffly.

"Is it time for our walk?" Alice asked. Constance might have been told that they were on their walk, but as yet, James had not been near Alice.

"I cannot today. It will be for the best if you find someone else to take you round the grounds from now on."

As this was the time they were completely alone and could enjoy kisses undisturbed, Alice was immediately concerned but could not be open with him whilst they were in company.

"I understand if you are busy, I thought you enjoyed the walks. I know I did," she said with a tentative smile. Something was wrong, and she had no idea what it was.

"It is best they stop. Good day." James turned on his heel and left the doorway.

"James!" Lady Kirkbride called after him, but he did not respond nor return.

***

"Something is amiss, and Constance is at the centre of it!" Lady Kirkbride raged to her husband after seeking him out in his study.

"We have known that Constance has been plotting from almost the moment Simon died, if not before," Baron Kirkbride responded.

"But why?" Lady Kirkbride almost wailed. "Simon was going to inherit from his uncle. I know he is still around, but surely he would help her and Cameron? Why could she not go on as before? Surely one upset was enough to inflict on us?"

"Seems the uncle did not like Constance's mercenary ways both before and after Simon died," Baron Kirkbride said. "That is why he insists the boy visit him, but Constance remains at home. I think for her compliance, she receives an allowance. She probably threatened to never let Cameron and his great-uncle meet if she was not provided for."

"I am not surprised at anything that girl will do, but I hate it when it involves my family."

"You have been very supportive of her. She would not have the run of the house as she does if it was not for your encouragement," the baron pointed out. "I have been surprised on more than one occasion that you let it continue, especially when James reacted negatively towards her. Surely your feelings of obligation ended then?"

Flopping into a chair in a most unladylike manner, Lady Kirkbride let out a long breath. "I know, and I cannot tell you how much I have regretted having her around, for I cannot like her no matter how hard I try, but there are other things going on." Not looking at her husband, she chewed her lip, an unusual action. The baron knew she was troubled but had no idea why. He would not force her to tell him her concerns but knew that when she was ready, she would turn to him.

"Your friendship with her mother?" he asked, offering his wife a way out of her discomfort.

"I admit that I felt sorry for her and wanted to maintain my friendship with Judith, but really, that girl just takes advantage of every situation and never thinks of anyone but herself." Lady Kirkbride looked relieved to have the subject no longer focused solely on her family.

"As Simon found out when they were married," Baron Kirkbride said dryly.

"I know," Lady Kirkbride said. "What he did to James was unforgivable, but he certainly paid for it. I never saw him smile once after he married Constance. I almost believe he willed himself to die as the only way he could escape her, and that is a terrible thing if my assumption is true, for the poor boy was certainly unhappy."

"You know she has James in her sights now, don't you?" Baron Kirkbride said gently.

"Of course I do! As the days go by, she is making it clearer and clearer. But he loves Miss Boyd, anyone can see it, and I am sure she is seething that James is no longer the malleable smitten boy he was when he left."

"Aye, he was in love with Miss Boyd before he even came home, and I would be glad to call her my daughter for she brings out the best in him."

"She does, and I have told her exactly that, but I think Constance has something up her sleeve, I just know it," Lady Kirkbride said in defeat.

"I have been expecting it every day since he returned," the baron acknowledged.

"Me too. What are we to do?"

"We take our lead from James," her husband said. "Whatever decisions he makes, we support him as always. I just hope he chooses happiness, for I do not know what Constance can offer that would sway him from Miss Boyd."

"He has a sense of honour which will be his undoing in all of this." Lady Kirkbride looked uncomfortable once more.

"We can only live in hope that he gets the happiness he deserves with the woman who deserves him."

Lady Kirkbride stood and went round the large desk to where her husband sat. Kissing his head, she smiled. “I love how you are still an old romantic after all these years.”

“Less of the old,” the baron said, swinging his wife round so that she was sitting on his knee. “How can I be anything but a romantic when you are my wife?”

“You say the nicest things.”

“Only to you, my love. Only to you.”

Chapter 9

Ben and Hamish returned late in the afternoon, immediately seeking out Alice. “It seems you were wrong about not having any letters,” Ben said. “There are three for you.”

“Perhaps they are from Archie?” Serena said excitedly.

“Probably telling me not to write another word.” Alice grimaced, but she tore open the first seal, eager to see what her brother had written. Without saying another word, she read the next two letters, and only then did she look up at the three people who were silently watching her. When she met their curious gazes, she smiled. “He has secured a publisher for me, and the publisher wants two further books as soon as possible.”

Serena was the first to reach Alice, and enveloping her in an embrace, she kissed her. “Congratulations and well deserved. I knew they would see your talent.”

“Thank you,” Alice said, clearly a little overwhelmed at the news.

Ben and Hamish both gave her their congratulations. "We shall be the first ones to buy copies," Ben said.

"Probably to try and work out if you appear in the book," Serena responded to her cousin.

"Of course. I hope I am the dashing hero," Ben responded.

"I have no doubt that in her next book you will find that I am the hero," Hamish said.

"You are both ridiculous," Serena chastised them.

"Miss Formby, I am wounded. I thought you were one of those fine ladies who recognised true perfection when they saw it."

Serena snorted. "I do, but I find none here, sir."

"Excuse my cousin, she has been too indulged by that club she belongs to and now feels she has the right to utter outrageous comments," Ben apologised.

"Comparing oneself to being perfect is a reasonable comment, is it? Then I am sorry for my naivete, but let us not forget this moment is not about either of you, it is about Alice."

"I am sorry, Miss Boyd." Hamish bowed. "Perhaps I would be better placed as the villain? I am sure they have more fun."

Alice had been watching the exchange with amusement and shared a smile with Serena. Hamish was everything that was charming and funny. She looked down once more at the letters. "It is so unbelievable. I never thought the first publisher Archie went to would accept it," Alice said, looking at the closely crossed pages as if they would disappear and she would find out it was some kind of joke.

"Not at all. We all knew you could do it. Just wait until the other Bluestockings find out. There will be a torrent of letters heading this way," Serena said.

"Archie says I have to return to London as soon as is possible. The publishers want me to sign contracts, and they have plans for me when the first book is published. They want me to do readings. In public."

"They are putting your name on the covers?" Serena asked in surprise. Some women did have their names on the books they had published, but in many cases gentlewomen chose to remain anonymous.

"They are willing to pay more if I will agree to it," Alice said. "Oh my word, I am to be paid for writing! I can hardly believe it."

"We shall leave you be," Ben said. "I can see you have a lot to take in, but congratulations, it is well deserved."

"Thank you," Alice said.

"If I see my brother, we will not utter a word, but I will send him to you," Hamish said.

"I would appreciate that."

When the two men had left, Alice let out a breath. "I never thought this would happen."

"Why not? We all know you are talented," Serena said.

"I am surrounded by wonderful friends who have never read a word I have written," Alice smiled.

"Yet," Serena said.

"I think the timing is typically poor," Alice said. "There is something amiss with Captain Avril, and I have to return to London."

"Are you fit to travel? You could send a message to explain about the accident. I am sure they would understand," Serena said.

"As long as I have help up any stairs and in and out of carriages, I will be fine," Alice assured her. "I want to stay, but know this is too good an opportunity to let pass. Archie urges me to return, saying it is vitally important."

"Of course you must go! We must go as soon as we are packed. Perhaps the besotted captain will join us as an escort?"

Alice laughed, but before she could reply, the door burst open and Drew entered the room. "Hamish has told me you are to be published! Is it true?"

"It is," Alice said.

"How many volumes are you to have? What will be the print run? Hold out for the highest amount for the copyright," Drew babbled, seeming almost as excited as Alice was.

"For someone who is determined to write because he cannot do anything else to rid himself of the inner turmoil, you certainly sound very business-minded," Alice said with a laugh.

Drew shrugged. "It is wise to be practical, and we all have to eat. I might want to be recognised for my talent, but I would like to earn enough to keep me alive. Only receiving accolades when you die must be so tiresome."

Serena smiled. "You are so young, and yet you sound far older than your years."

"I am often overlooked," Drew said. "That does not mean to say that when I have something to say, it is not important."

"That is very true, and I need to travel to London exactly for the reasons you have mentioned," Alice said.

"You are leaving then?" James's voice came from where he stood in the doorway. For someone so large, he could move with stealth. He looked troubled and terribly sad; there was no sign of his usual gruffness.

"Of course she is. Fame and fortune await her in the capital, just as it does for all of us who are blessed with the talent of storytelling," Drew said dramatically.

"Drew, we need to leave your brother and Miss Boyd to have a chat," Serena said.

"But I want to know the details the publisher is offering," Drew said.

"And I am sure it will be all that is talked about for days to come. Please come with me."

Drew looked fit to argue but then, looking between Alice and James, he sighed. "The road is never smooth, is it?"

Serena smiled at him. "I am sure it will get easier at some point. I would like to see some of your poetry if you are willing to share it with me."

"Oh yes, come to the library. I have bound my own booklet," Drew said, distracted enough to leave James and Alice alone.

James stepped into the room, and though he smiled at Alice, she detected real unhappiness in his eyes. "I could return here after I am no longer needed in London," she said quietly. "I do not have to stay for long."

"I knew the first publisher who read your work would grab the chance to work with you." There was real pride in his voice, and it lifted Alice's spirits a little, for at his entrance, he had seemed unreachable.

"Thank you. We could go to London together," she suggested, a blush tinging her cheeks at being forward. "It would not seem so unusual as I was the one who chased after you. It would be nice for you to be there with me. I would even let you travel in the same carriage."

James looked as if to sit by her but then changed his mind at the last minute and sat in a chair opposite her. "I cannae go to London nor anywhere else."

"I do not have to go. You mean more to me than my book does." Alice saw the flinch her words caused. "What is it, James? What has gone wrong? You were asking me to marry you by special licence not too long ago, and now you appear to want to be a hundred miles from me."

"I wish we had got that special licence," James mumbled, half to himself, before looking at Alice. "I am sorry, everything has changed. You need to go to London, carve out a new life for yourself, one which does not involve me."

"What? No!" Alice went to move off the sofa, but James jumped from his seat and put even more distance between them. She winced as her foot twinged at her sudden movement, but though he had always come to her aid in the past, this time he remained at a distance from her. "James, what has happened? I need the truth from you. This is not about me needing to go to London, is it? Something else is amiss, and I need to know what it is."

James shook his head, unable to speak as he watched the woman he loved realise that he was not going to give her anything of what he had promised.

"This has to do with Constance, doesn't it?" Alice asked quietly. Tears filled her eyes, though she tried to blink them away. She would not show weakness in front of him; she would not be that insipid watering pot. "I will never be convinced that you have rediscovered the affection you had for each other because I know you enough to see that you can hardly bear to be in her company. Have the decency to tell me the truth. Please, James, I need to know whatever it is."

"I am so sorry, Alice. Please believe that if there was anything I could do to change this damned situation, I would, lassie," James said, almost reaching out for her but rubbing his hand through his hair instead. "The boy is mine."

"Boy? Who? Oh, her son," Alice said, suddenly realising with his one short sentence that Constance had won.

"Yes, and if I do not recognise him, she will cause as much trouble as she can," James said.

"You laid with her?" she asked on a whisper.

"Not that I remember, but she insists we did." The pain on Alice's face at his words cut him deeper than any cut he had received on the battlefield.

"But she has brought him up as Simon's son. No one would condemn you for not believing her." Alice was grasping at straws, she knew she was, but she could not go without a fight, though in her heart she knew it was in vain. He would stand by a child he thought he had created, even though he could not be completely sure it was his.

"That is true and was my first reaction," James assured her. "From the little of her you have seen, you will have gathered that Constance is not going to give up without a fight. She has threatened to spread all sorts of rumours about how my family and I have treated her. A lot of it will not stick, nor be believed, but some of it will. I have Ma, Mary and Drew to think of."

"She might not." Alice knew without doubt that her words were said out of desperation, for even with such a short acquaintance, Constance was the type of woman with no scruples if it benefited her, and she clearly wanted James. At least Alice could understand that part of her motivation.

"I cannae take that risk when it involves my family, particularly with regards to Mary and Drew, and she knows that."

"She also knows you are honourable and would never abandon a child," Alice said.

"It is true, I could not and believe me that at this moment I wish I could walk away and join you in London, forgetting everything I have been told, but there is a small chance that she is telling the truth and he could be my son."

"You would never be happy if you left now, and as much as it breaks my heart, I meant what I said at Hesketh Hall. I will never accept being second best, and returning to London with me after hearing about the boy, your heart would still be here."

"One thing is certain, Alice, wherever you are is where my heart will be. You said I should come home to sort out my feelings, and it was clear from almost the first time I saw Constance that I felt nothing for her; I was lamenting over a memory that was not real. It does not alter the fact that I cannae abandon him, or her for that matter," James tried to explain when all he wanted to do was take her in his arms and kiss the pain away for her. For him. For them both. He was convinced that he would never smile or feel happiness again.

"I know you cannot. It is part of the reason I love you," Alice said sadly.

"Please. Do not say that. I am sorry, which is a feeble thing to say after what has happened. You know I am not one for spouting words that can express what needs to be said, but I cannot let you torture us both by voicing your feelings. You know I feel the same, but it is of no use."

Alice laughed a hollow laugh. "No, it is Drew's talent to give long, impassioned speeches, not you.

Please could you send someone to carry me upstairs? I would like to return to my chamber. For once, I cannot allow you to carry me."

"Let me take you," James said, stepping towards her, but he stopped when Alice put up her hand.

"No. Let me try to hold on to my dignity. If you touch me, I shall lose all reason, and it will not be a pretty sight, for I refuse to beg for what I want," she said, the tears she had tried so hard to hold back streaming down her face.

"I am sorry, Alice. I truly wish things could have been different. Goodbye." James walked out of the room, barking an order to a footman, who came and assisted Alice to her chamber and sent for Serena without being instructed to.

When Serena entered the room, she rushed to Alice's side. "What is it? What has happened?" she asked as her friend sobbed uncontrollably into her pillow.

Alice could not speak, nor could she stop crying. Serena took hold of her and rocked her for an hour before Alice managed to stop her outpouring of grief. Hiccupping sobs were the only sound in the room, but Serena did not press her friend for any information or explanation, she just continued to rock her and stroke her hair.

Eventually Alice's eyes fluttered shut, and when Serena was sure she was in a deep but troubled sleep, she lay her down, remained with her until she was certain that she would not wake immediately and left the room.

Finding Ben and Hamish in the billiard room, they stopped their game as soon as she entered. "Stopped celebrating already?" Ben asked.

"We need to leave," Serena said.

"Why? I know Alice said she was needed in London, but surely there is no desperate hurry?" Ben asked in some surprise.

"I am sorry to be so disparaging about your brother, sir, but he has treated Alice poorly. I have not the details to know what has gone on, but after having a conversation with him, she is more upset than I have ever seen her, and she has never been a wet goose," Serena said, her tone and posture of haughty indignation.

"Blast it. What has the fool done?" Hamish said, putting his cue down. "Has he refused to go to London with her?"

"I doubt the normally stoic Alice would be utterly bereft if that was the case. Something else has happened," Serena responded, at which Ben nodded.

"She is no flighty woman who acts out dramatics. She is very sensible," Ben said to Hamish.

"In that case I can only apologise for the stupidity of my brother," Hamish said. "Should I seek him out?"

"I doubt it will do any good," Serena said. "She could not utter anything to tell me what had gone on between them, but I do think it would be of benefit to her if we were to leave as soon as can be arranged."

"Stay until the morning," Hamish said. "It is late now; you would only be able to travel a few miles before losing the light completely. If she is asleep, let her be and start off on the morrow. I shall be sorry to see you all go, but I understand your need to leave and can only curse my brother for being a coxcomb."

"Thank you," Ben said. "He is right, Serena. We will set off at first light."

Serena nodded in agreement. "I will seek out Lady Kirkbride before returning to Alice. Your mother has been nothing but welcoming and kind. I am sorry it is ending so suddenly and with so much upset."

"She will be sorry to see you go, we all will," Hamish responded. When Serena left the room, he started to roll his shirt sleeves down and shrug himself into his frock coat. "I think I need to seek out my brother. He is clearly not thinking straight to have upset Miss Boyd so much. Sometimes family can be a blasted bore."

"I would advise him to stay away from Serena. She has a fair punch on her when she is angry, and I could almost see sparks flying from her eyes," Ben said.

"Oh, do not worry. He will not be seeking anyone out when I have finished with him," Hamish said grimly.

Chapter 10

"What the devil do you think you are about, damn you!" Hamish spat at his brother the moment he marched into his chamber. "I should give you the beating of your life."

"Leave it," James replied, not moving from the bed where he sat.

"Leave it? Since when do you go around breaking the hearts of innocents? That is the type of thing I do, not you. You are the honourable one."

James snorted with derision. "And being the stupid fool who always has to do the right thing has landed me in this blasted mess."

"You had better start talking, brother, because at the moment I want to punch you until you cry," Hamish said.

"The way I am feeling now, I will not need a single punch to start my tears."

Hamish propped himself on the edge of the bed, realising there was something seriously amiss with James. "What has happened, brother?"

"Constance."

"You cannot surely be classing her as a better life partner than..."

"Good grief! No! I have come to the conclusion that it was the infatuation of youth that attracted me to her."

"I can accept that. She can make herself very pleasing when she wants to," Hamish said.

James raised an eyebrow. "Tried her wiles on you, did she?"

"Oh yes, a long time ago and only briefly, but I am made of stronger stuff than most when it comes to conniving women." Hamish grinned.

"Seems you had a lucky escape. I have not been so lucky."

"Tell me what she has done." Hamish had never seen his brother look so desolate, and he had seen him when he had found out that Constance and Simon had betrayed him. He had never expected James to suffer more than he had then, but it was clear that was nothing compared to what he was feeling now. Hamish could only wonder what Constance had done.

James swung his legs off the bed and strode to the door. "There is no point. What's done is done, and there is no changing the course I am on now. I will never stop loving Alice, but I cannae be with her. If anyone wants me, I will be in the forest."

"It is almost night."

"I will return when Alice's party has left. I cannae see again the pain in her eyes showing just how much I have hurt her," James said, walking out of his chamber, leaving Hamish behind.

"Blast Constance," Hamish cursed, following his brother out of the room.

***

The removal of the visiting party was done with much sadness on all sides. Mary begged Alice and Serena to keep in touch, but as she embraced Alice for the last time, she grimaced at her. “You will not write, I know that, and part of me does not blame you, but I wish you would.”

Alice smiled sadly. “I promise to try; just give me a little time.”

“I will. I am going to miss you both so much,” Mary said, embracing Serena.

“We will miss you too, and if you ever travel to London, you must meet the Bluestockings and we shall take you out and about,” Serena said.

Mary smiled. “I would like that, almost enough to take me to London.”

“But not quite?” Serena asked.

“Not quite.”

“It is time to go,” Ben said. “We need to make good progress; our famous author needs to make an appointment with her publisher.”

They all knew it was not the real story that the party needed to leave quite so soon, but it was convenient for them to believe that the urgency to meet the publisher was the only reason for the hurried departure. It did not lift the mood any, just enabled everyone not to be too awkward around each other.

Alice was embraced by both Baron and Lady Kirkbride, each apologising to her without knowing quite what they were apologising for. Drew was more pragmatic about the situation, giving Alice advice until she climbed into the carriage.

As it drew away, Baron Kirkbride turned to his son. "I always thought you would be the starving poet, but after hearing you giving out business advice, I am now reassured that you will go far, my boy."

"I study the newspapers too, Da," Drew said. "I know what is needed to be done to get a good publishing deal, there are rogues out there, and I can only hope that Miss Boyd looks into her contract as I have advised. I would not get taken in as others have been."

"I am glad to hear it. I think I might start to seek you out when I am making business decisions of my own."

Drew looked pleased. "Anytime, Da." He waved at the group as he rushed into the house and up the stairs, clearly pleased with receiving praise from his father.

The rest of the family moved towards the door, but a movement from the side of the house made them pause. James walked around the corner, purposely not looking down the drive at the departing carriage.

"Son?" Baron Kirkbride said gently.

"Whilst you are all here, I want to tell you that I shall be marrying Constance whenever we can arrange it. She has gone to collect Cameron, and he will be living with us, no longer staying with Simon's uncle," James said.

"Oh, James!" Lady Kirkbride moaned.

"No, Ma. Not another word. I know what you will all think, and I assure you I feel it all and more, but the deed is done. I have to take responsibility for my actions when I was young and foolish. They have well and truly caught up with me, and I will not have my honour or the respect of this family put into question because of my stupidity." James walked into the house and went into the library, and closing the door with a bang, he left his family looking at each other.

"She has got her way," Lady Kirkbride said.

"Can someone please tell me what the devil is going on and why James is marrying a doxy? How has she convinced him to marry her when he loves Miss Boyd?" Mary asked.

"Mind your language, young lady!" Lady Kirkbride scolded her daughter. "You were at school when most of it happened. I had hoped it would remain in the past, but I had not taken into account the determination of Constance though I have tried to indulge her to keep her happy. I am going to visit Judith and try to get her to have a talk with Constance."

"Tread carefully, my dear. You know how protective Judith is of Constance," the baron cautioned.

"I have spent the last few years being careful and trying to keep the peace and look how that turned out, my middle boy more distraught than when he discovered how Simon had betrayed him. I am reaching the end of my tether, and if Judith should utter a word out of turn, she will feel the full force of my feelings," Lady Kirkbride said of Constance's mother.

"I do not know if I would like to see that confrontation or not," Hamish said.

"I am not that brave," Mary said.

"Nor I," Baron Kirkbride said as they entered the house together.

***

Constance was gone over a sennight, which everyone hoped was a sign that she had changed her mind, but after ten days news reached them that she had returned and her son was with her. The mood in the Kirkbride house lowered at the news, but James refused to talk about possible ways out of the situation.

His response was always the same. "I will not have this family's name dragged through the mud because of my actions."

After a day, Constance arrived at the Kirkbride home, and for the first time she did not walk into the house but allowed herself to be announced.

Mary and Lady Kirkbride looked up in surprise as the footman stepped back after undertaking the formalities.

"Why, Constance, this is not your usual way of arriving," Lady Kirkbride said, but she was no longer as welcoming as she had been, which Constance noticed immediately.

"I know, but I thought that until I have the right to live here, perhaps a little formality would not go amiss," Constance said, not waiting to be invited to sit, just sitting down.

"You are to live here?" Mary asked in shock.

"But of course." Constance smiled at her. "Where else would we live?"

"In a cottage on the estate?" Lady Kirkbride asked faintly.

"Oh no, for I am sure the baron would prefer to have James close at hand. We all know how flighty Hamish is, so for the future of the family, it is important that James provides a steady support to his father."

"You do know that Hamish will inherit, whether James lives under this roof or not," Mary pointed out sharply.

"Clearly I do, for he lords it around the area as if he is already Lord Kirkbride. It might be an idea to have a quiet word in his ear, my lady," Constance said to Lady Kirkbride. "It does not reflect well on him to appear keen to take over the mantle of baron."

"Well... I-I never!" Lady Kirkbride stuttered.

"Do not worry, Ma. Can I call you Ma? I feel we might as well dispense with formalities because it will not be long before you are officially Ma to me. I am prepared to take my role as second woman of importance in the family very seriously, and you can give me any tasks you feel are getting too much for you. In fact I insist," Constance said with a smile. "Let me start by ordering tea."

Even Mary appeared dumbfounded at the way Constance had taken over their morning, and she could not think of a retort, her mind full of the horror of having Constance under the same roof. Eventually, she looked at her mother. "Ma, I think I need a season in London after all."

"Oh, sister, no!" Constance trilled. "You are far too old for a season; you should have gone the year you left the school room. You must be two and twenty now, far beyond the age of trying to secure a beau. I am sure we could find you someone suitable in the area, more than likely a widower."

"If you think I would let you interfere with my getting a husband, you do not know me so well," Mary responded tartly. "Some of us have a conscience and refuse to trick others into marriage."

The smiling façade dipped for a few moments as Constance glared at Mary, but it returned when James walked in. He faltered slightly as if deciding whether to turn tail and leave, but his shoulders sagged in defeat when Constance stood to greet him.

"James, I have missed you!" Crossing the room, she kissed his cheek. "We have lots to talk about and arrange."

"Where is the boy?" James asked gruffly.

"He is with my mother. I thought it best to let him rest for a day or two whilst we sort out the wedding details."

"I would like to meet him."

"Of course you will. I have not told him yet about you and our union. He was so upset at losing Simon that I thought it best for him to get to know you first, and then we can tell him that you are to be his da."

"You seem to be managing everyone," Mary said.

"It is something I am good at."

"Aren't you just."

"Mary," Lady Kirkbride warned.

"I am only agreeing with my sister," Mary defended herself.

"Do not worry. Mary and I will become the best of friends," Constance assured Lady Kirkbride. "Come, James, let us have a stroll around the gardens while we talk. I have ordered tea, but I can order some fresh when we return."

Without looking at what effect her words had on the group, she took hold of James's arm and led him out of the room.

"Ma, something has to be done!" Mary appealed to her parent.

"It is going to be worse than I could ever imagine," Lady Kirkbride almost moaned the words.

"She will ruin this family and destroy James. I have never seen him so defeated," Mary said, accepting the tea tray which was brought in. Neither woman felt like having anything from the tray. It was almost as if they did, they would be admitting that Constance had indeed taken over their lives.

"I know, but your father insists that it up to James to fix," Lady Kirkbride said once the footman had left.

"How can we abandon him when he has lost the will to do anything?"

"I cannot think of a way of stopping the marriage, but I will be speaking to your father. You are right in that we must not sit idly by whilst she takes over our lives," Lady Kirkbride said. "I have tolerated her inappropriate behaviour, but it was nothing to how she has been the last two times of seeing her. I shall move out to one of the cottages if she gets her way and lives in the main house."

"I think that would suit her perfectly, then she would become lady of the manor. I wonder why she has not tried to gain Hamish's favour?" Mary mused. "He is to be the next baron."

"With Constance, I would not be surprised at anything she does anymore."

Chapter 11

James shook off Constance's arm the moment they stepped outside, and although he walked alongside her, he made sure they did not touch.

"There is no point being missish," Constance teased. "We are to be man and wife in every sense of the word."

"Not if I can help it," James growled out. "You may have forced me into agreeing to marry you, but that will be in name only. I said I will not lay with you, and I meant it."

"No, no, no." Constance smiled at him. "I know you are hankering after your writer now, which I will allow for a little while, but let me be clear, this is a marriage in the truest sense, or the deal is off."

James swung round to face her. "Deal? Deal? You are speaking as if I had a part in this farce. I will never lay with you, take it or leave it. At this point, I do not care either way."

Anger flittered over Constance's features, but her voice remained calm. "If you are willing to be guided by me, in the end you will have more than just a son to be thankful for."

“I have no idea what schemes you are planning, but stop it now,” James said, starting to walk again. It was a little comfort that at least if he was walking beside her, he did not have to look at her.

“If we continue to pretend that Cameron is Simon’s son and allow him to visit Simon’s uncle regularly, the man will still leave his fortune to Cameron. When the old man dies, we can tell Cameron the truth, and by then it will not matter; our son will have a fortune far larger than he could inherit from either of us.”

“But it would be obtained deceitfully,” James pointed out.

Constance waved her hand in dismissal. “The uncle will be happy and Cameron will benefit; there is no harm done. It means we have one less thing to worry about.”

“What else is there of concern?”

“Your mother suggested we live in a cottage in the grounds, but I have told her that we will live in the main house. I also think the sooner Mary is married off the better, and Drew needs to be sent to school or apprenticed somewhere. At least he can learn something useful instead of mooning about the place,” Constance said.

“You are trying to manage the whole of my family!” James exclaimed in shock. “Are you not satisfied that I have agreed to your terms? Why interfere with their lives?”

“Hamish is the head of the family for the moment and is doing nothing apart from being a wastrel. You need to make sure that everything is to our satisfaction, for he will not stir himself to ensure we are provided for."

"You said Hamish is the head of the family, but you are forgetting yourself. My father is very much alive and in good health. It is up to him and only him to manage my brothers and sister," James snapped.

"I am very fond of your father," Constance said. "The chance of Hamish inheriting is very slim, is it not? The way his life is full of dissipation and heady pursuits. It will be a miracle if he reaches thirty."

"Your aim is to be Lady Kirkbride?"

The incredulous tone of voice was not lost on Constance, and she bristled with anger. "Of course it is, and with very little effort on our part, it should be easy to achieve. You must want it too. After all, if you become baron, that means Cameron will inherit after your death."

"You are unbelievable!" James spat. "Tell me, was this your idea from the very start, before I went to war?"

"It is not an unreasonable plan to have," Constance said, completely unrepentant at her ambitions being in the open.

"There are so many points that are either ridiculous or slightly sinister that I am concerned about your sanity at this moment."

"Do not think that you can have me locked away!" Constance snarled at James, all pleasantries gone. "There is a letter in a safe place that states that you have been planning to get rid of me and the reasons why."

"Let me guess, none of which reflects badly on you," James said sarcastically.

"Of course not. My plans were always to benefit us," Constance said, smile in place once more.

"Tell me, when did you try to get Hamish interested in you? Was it before we got together or after I left for war?" James demanded.

"As soon as you told me you were leaving."

"Do you know something, Constance, I never thought it would happen, but I actually feel sorry for Simon, for he must have been taken in by you as much as I was. Did he ever realise that he had made a mistake?"

"He married me because he loved me!" Constance snapped. "Just as you would have done."

"Yes, I would, but I realise now that it would have been a rude awakening. I wonder how soon after you got Simon to marry you did he realise his mistake? I suppose the advantage I have is that at least I know your true character before we are wed. What little comfort that is."

"You can walk away if you like. No one is forcing you to marry me."

James laughed. "And you know I will not abandon a child of mine nor put my family through a scandal or embarrassment. You hit on the perfect scheme for me to comply with your demands."

"In that case, you can start giving me the respect your wife deserves," Constance said.

"Fine, betrothed. Bring my son tomorrow, or I will come to you."

"You had better be gentle with him. I will not have you frightening him like the monster you are."

"The monster you are prepared to spend the rest of your life with," James said dryly.

"Sometimes we have to make sacrifices to get what we want."

"You disgust me," James said, turning on his heel and walking away from his wife-to-be.

***

Hamish found James, drunk, in the library. "Ah damn! We thought you had seen sense and run away. All your family will be disappointed to find you are still here."

"I thought I was still in love with Constance. Why did I fall for her charms in the first place? Did she ever even have any charm? I am beginning to think it was all an act," James slurred.

"The years have not mellowed her but made her more of the mercenary than she was when she set her sights on you," Hamish said, filling a glass of whiskey and sitting opposite his brother.

"She is certainly that. After we are wed and she moves in here, I would watch your step every time you walk downstairs. After the conversation I have had with her today, I do not think she will be happy until I am next in line for the title."

Hamish smiled slightly. "Duly noted."

"Did you not fall for her even slightly when she approached you? In a strange way, I think it would go some way to reassure me if you did."

"I have many faults, dear brother, but taking the woman my brother has proclaimed to be his life partner is not something I would ever consider doing, even if she was the diamond of the season."

"Sorry, of course you would not. My thoughts are all over the place. I suppose I am just trying to figure out a way out of this mess, when in reality if I do, I will be turning my back on my son, and I cannae do that. Though it gives Constance all the power."

"She has said the boy is yours?" Hamish asked in surprise.

"Yes."

"Do you believe her?"

"Part of me does, part of me hopes it is wrong, then I have an escape." James shrugged, taking another large swig of his drink and holding out his glass for Hamish to refill it. "That is the coward's way. I have to stand by the child until the rich uncle dies and leaves him his fortune, then we can tell him that I am his father," he finished as Hamish poured the liquid into his glass. "I do not think there is enough whiskey in Scotland to wipe out what I am feeling."

"She certainly has thought of everything," Hamish mused.

"Hasn't she? I know Alice was right in saying that I needed to sort out my past, but I did not think this would be the result, finding out my true feelings and then having my heart ripped out."

"Miss Boyd is correct in one regard," Hamish said.

"What is that?"

"We are a family prone to the dramatics."

James laughed into his glass, but his chuckle turned into a strangled sob. "I will never see her again and I cannot bear it."

"Let us deal with one thing at a time, brother. You are not married to Constance yet."

"I refuse to get my hopes up when turning my back on her could mean I am turning my back on my child."

"There are still things we can do. Constance has had too much influence in this family, and I still do not quite understand why, but I think by working together we can make sure she understands where she fits in this family," Hamish said.

"I admire your optimism, but apparently you are going to die, as is Father. Mary is going to be married off, preferably to a widower, and Drew is to be apprenticed."

Hamish let out a crack of laughter, making James smile for the first time in days. "No! She cannot have uttered those words!" Hamish spluttered, unable to stop chuckling.

"Oh yes she did," James confirmed.

"I do like a challenge. Now I am determined to try and catch her out, for someone who weaves so many situations cannot keep all her lies contained. One day she is going to make a mistake, and we will be there to revel in it."

"I hope you are right, for I have half a mind to throw myself off a mountain," James said, emptying his glass. "The only thing stopping me is the fact that I would probably survive and be so badly injured that I could do nothing but sit and watch Constance's machinations for the remainder of my days."

"Have a little faith, brother. You are not leg-shackled quite yet."

James stumbled to the door before turning. "I would appreciate it if you and the rest of the family would be there when I meet the boy tomorrow."

"Of course, if you wish it."

"She commands that we do not tell him he is mine so that he can get his fortune, but if he is my son, I will be saying so as soon as I meet him. I refuse to let her have her own way on everything."

"Bravo! That is the James we all love. I shall look forward to tomorrow, now go and sleep the whiskey off. We need you clear-headed if you are going to explain the reality of my nephew's heritage to him and the rest of the family."

"Bloody hell. I have a son. What are Ma and Da going to feel when they know what I did?" James asked, walking through the door and heading to his chamber, lucid enough to know that Hamish was right; he had to be prepared for tomorrow.

Chapter 12

London

It had been a whirl of meetings, editing and approvals since almost the moment Alice's feet had touched the ground, well, one foot, as she still could not put any weight on her injured ankle.

Having obtained her own invalid chair, Alice was grateful to her Bluestocking friends who escorted her to the appointments she needed to attend.

Now, she stood in front of them, cheeks aflame, book in hand, trying to read an excerpt. "I keep stammering and stuttering," she moaned for the fifth time in as many minutes. "How am I going to read anything to a roomful of strangers?"

"It could be that it is harder to read to us as you know us so well," Grace, the founder of the Bluestocking Club and somewhat of a mother hen to the others, consoled her. "I think you are worrying too much."

"Why does the publisher think that it is something people want to take part in, listening to only a small part of the book from the author who has chosen a solitary profession because she does not like people!" Alice said.

Her friends laughed, knowing that Alice was very sociable in her own quiet way, but Lydia, the friend who had created the soldier's retreat, took pity on her.

"This is doing you no good. Leave it now, and tomorrow just stand up and speak and then depart. If it does not go well, the publisher will never ask you to do another, and if they love you as we do, you will sell lots of books and make more money!"

Alice laughed. "Thank you, I think. You are right about one thing, I cannot do this in front of you all. Please do not attend tomorrow's reading."

"But we have tickets!" Serena said.

"I will pay you back for them," Alice said. "I just know if I see one of your faces, however encouraging, my mouth will stop working."

"We would never make you feel more uncomfortable than you already do," Grace said. "You will not see us."

"Thank you." Alice sat down with relief. "Publishing is not what I expected."

"It will get easier," Serena assured her.

Grace decided it was time to take Alice's mind off her troubles. "I am going to visit Arabella in a few days; she has asked for my help." Her words were the perfect distraction.

"Arabella?"

"She is asking for a visit?"

"Something must be amiss!"

"Is she ill?"

The questions made Grace laugh and hold her hands up in defeat. "No, she is not ill, yes, she has asked me to visit, and all she said was that although everything was well with her, she needed my help with something. You know she never writes long letters."

"Yes, I usually get three lines; she is well, no, she does not need anything, and she hopes all is well with me," Julia, Lady Bryn, said with a smile.

"Me too," came the chorus of voices.

"It is still early days after the accident, relatively speaking," Grace said of the most beautiful of their group, who had suffered greatly after a carriage accident.

"I am glad she survived, however distant she is now," Alice said. "I hope that one day she will feel able to join us once more."

"I think with patience she will do, or at least be able to accept visitors," Grace said.

"You are the first to go since she was well enough to demand that we all leave," Serena said of the time they had been cast out of Arabella's home, with thanks and embraces, but very firmly told to leave and only return when invited.

"Yes, to say she could barely sit up, she could make her views known very clearly," Grace said. "There must have been some progress if she wants me to visit."

"We should give you letters for her," Julia said.

"And presents, we know how she liked the bonbons she would overindulge with every time she passed her favourite shop," Lydia said.

"I will be leaving in three days, so gather whatever you wish to send with me," Grace said.

"I am surprised you are not going straight away," Lydia said. "Three days gives her plenty of time to send a withdrawal of the invitation."

Serena laughed. "That would be so like her!"

"I replied and said the reason I was staying was to make sure Alice was happy after her public displays, and I assured Arabella that I would be travelling to see her even if she rescinded her invitation, which she has done in the past. I have not had a response, so I am hoping she has understood that I will not be put off." Grace smiled at the laughter her words caused.

***

Alice wiped sweaty hands along her muslin gown. Her heartbeat was so loud she was sure the audience would be able to hear it. Licking her lips to try to relieve the dryness in her mouth, she turned to her publisher, Mr Mortimer. "This is going to be a disaster."

"Not at all. Everyone in the room has paid to come and hear you. They are on your side, Miss Boyd."

"Until I open my mouth and ruin their illusion."

He patted her hand in reassurance. "Trust me, I would not be risking my reputation if I was not confident that you would go out there and impress them all."

"Thank you, you have just managed to add more pressure than I was already feeling," Alice moaned.

"Looks like all the chairs are filled and everyone is settled. It is time for me to introduce you."

Mr Mortimer walked onto the little stage which was at the front of the rows of chairs. The room was used as a gathering place rather than a theatre as it only held about a hundred people. He was happy that all the tickets had been sold and even a few extra had been bought for those who did not mind standing at the back.

As he spoke of Alice's work and what had attracted him to the story, at the back of the room, Lydia whispered to Grace. "You do realise that if she sees us, she will never forgive us."

"We are on the last row. There are more bonnets between us and the stage than you would see if the Regent was here," Grace whispered back.

Julia choked on a laugh. "I think I might permanently damage my back through slouching in my seat for too long. My mother would have a fit if she were still alive and could see my appalling posture."

Alice came onto the stage, looking terrified, silencing her friends as they all inwardly wished for her to be a success. After a slightly stumbled start, Alice seemed to gather herself and stood more confidently, her voice carrying across the room. She added inflections when needed, pausing to add drama and smiled when the words that were meant to cause amusement were greeted with laughter. At the end of the excerpt she had chosen to read, there was much applause and then she answered questions. It was surprising how many seemed eager to follow the same route as Alice, and no one made any comment about a gentlewoman making a living or it being a bad thing. They all seem to have been impressed with her talent.

Eventually the questions were brought to a close by Mr Mortimer, and Alice was allowed to mingle with her audience with her publisher by her side while Mr Mortimer's assistant sold books to those who had not already bought them.

Alice's friends stood towards the back of the room but were no longer trying to hide themselves from Alice's view. It was not long before she spotted them and came over, smiling ruefully at them.

"I knew you would come," she said, accepting embraces and congratulations from the group.

"We were not going to miss such a momentous day," Julia said. "Although if it all went wrong, we were going to blame Grace."

Shaking her head at Julia, Grace turned to Alice. "If you had as much faith in yourself as you do in others, there would not have been any nerves on your part."

"Oh, I do not have faith in everyone, not anymore at least. I have learned a hard lesson in that regard," Alice said. She smiled at Serena, who squeezed her arm in silent support, but Alice carried on speaking. "I am glad you were here, though. Thank you for coming."

Mr Mortimer approached the group, having left her side when Alice had said that the group were her friends. "Sorry to interrupt, ladies, but there is a guest who would particularly like to speak to Miss Boyd."

"Of course," Grace murmured. "We shall meet up tomorrow and you can tell us everything," she said to Alice.

Walking away, Mr Mortimer whispered to Alice. "Prepare yourself, Miss Boyd. It is Lady Sefton who wishes to be introduced to you."

Alice flashed her publisher a look of alarm. "*The* Lady Sefton? Of Almack's?"

"The one and the same," Mr Mortimer said.

"I did not realise she was here."

"Nor I, but it is wonderful that she has stayed behind and wishes to be introduced to you. She must have been very impressed."

Alice wasn't as sure as her publisher was that it was a wonderful thing, as her hands became sweaty once more with nerves, but it was certainly an honour. One of the top ladies of the *ton* was asking to make her acquaintance, a bluestocking and published author, two facts that would normally have the most influential and popular people avoiding her. One day she would wake from this dream, but for now she could not help but enjoy the wonder of it all, even though she was extremely nervous.

Mr Mortimer made the introductions and then stepped away so as not to intrude on the conversation, that it was done as a result of a look of dismissal Lady Sefton had given him was even more daunting for

Alice. Though Lady Sefton was known to be one of the kinder of the patronesses, she was still a woman with a huge amount of influence in society.

"My dear, I am so pleased to meet you. Your writing reminds me so much of the early work of Fanny Burney. It was a joy to listen to it being read."

"Thank you, my lady. You are very kind. I can only aspire to have such a way with words as someone like Mrs Burney has."

"Do not be too modest. We all know how quickly fashions change and people fall out of favour, you need to make your money while you can," Lady Sefton said with a mischievous look.

Alice laughed despite her nerves. "I hope I do not fall out of fashion quite so quickly, for my publisher has commissioned two more novels."

"Excellent! I see he is an astute businessman," Lady Sefton said, glancing at Mr Mortimer, who was still hovering a discreet distance away. "My friends would not accompany me today, they can be irritating sometimes with their self-importance, but it seems I am stuck with them. I am determined that they would enjoy meeting you and wish you to come to tea with the patronesses and do a reading for us in private. You will obviously have my recommendation after today, but if you want to sell in vast quantities to the *ton*, having the ladies of Almack's recommending you will guarantee sales. Although it can be seen as vulgar to speak about money, we both know it is what everyone is bothered about, and I think you deserve to be rewarded when you have produced such entertaining words."

"Oh, my lady, that would be an honour, but I have to admit that the thought of performing in front of you all is slightly terrifying."

Lady Sefton laughed, drawing curious looks from those around them. "I like you, Miss Boyd, and you will win them over, just as you did with everyone today. I shall send round the details of when you can join us, and your reward will be a ticket for Almack's and lots of book sales, of course." Lady Sefton smiled at her. "Do not tell my friends, but if I was you, the book sales would excite me more than an evening drinking lemonade at Almack's. One has to carry out one's duties, though, and it is the place to be seen, so perhaps you will enjoy it just a little."

Alice curtseyed, thanking her benefactor as Lady Sefton departed. As Alice watched her in disbelief, she was approached by her parents.

"Oh Alice, you were perfect!" Mrs Boyd gushed. "And it seems you made an impression on Lady Sefton! How wonderful!"

"Am I in some kind of dream?" Alice asked.

"I would think all your dreams have been answered," Mr Boyd said.

Alice grimaced. "Not quite all." She had not been able to move the feeling of lead in her stomach since she had left the Highlands, no matter how much her publishing dreams were coming to fruition.

Squeezing his daughter's hand, he smiled sadly at her, knowing to what she referred. She had a close relationship with her parents and kept no secrets from them. "It is his loss," he said quietly.

"One day, I hope to believe you," Alice said, but she inwardly shook herself. Now was not the time for repining, she had experienced something exhilarating, and she was not going to let thoughts of James spoil it, though she thought of little else. She would force herself to enjoy today, for it was all she had hoped for until he had turned her world upside down.

Mr Mortimer returned to Alice's side after being approached by his assistant, who whispered something in his ear. "If you would excuse my interruption, I thought you would like to know that we have sold out of the books we brought today. I am going to speak to my partner tomorrow and suggest that we start another print run; sales have been going very well."

"That is good news!" Mr Boyd said.

"If you would allow me to call on you tomorrow, Miss Boyd, I shall update you on our decision, and if I might be so bold, I would be honoured if you would join me on a carriage ride and perhaps a stop at Gunter's for some ices?" Mr Mortimer was blushing furiously, making it clear that this was not a purely business arrangement.

"Oh, that would be— Yes, yes, of course," Alice said, looking embarrassed.

"Wonderful! I will collect you at three of the clock if that is acceptable?"

"Yes, perfectly fine."

"Excellent. Until tomorrow, Miss Boyd." Mr Mortimer bowed and returned to his assistant before leaving the venue.

"Well! That was a surprise," Mrs Boyd said to the still blushing Alice.

"Not really," Mr Boyd said. "Have you not noticed how he has been watching her and hovering close all the time?"

"I thought that was because he was her publisher and was looking after his interests," Mrs Boyd answered.

"Then you are not as romantic as I, for I could see clearly the affection in his eyes. Perhaps this is a good thing in all respects?" Mr Boyd said, turning to Alice. "A man who has your best interests at heart and who understands your need to work. He seems pleasant too, and though I know little of these things, I think he would be considered handsome?"

Alice did not reply but watched Mr Mortimer depart. He was an attractive man, only about thirty, so clearly capable enough to have his own successful business at a relatively young age. He had been very attentive since they had met, but… Alice just could not help comparing him to James, and there was no comparison.

James did everything 'big'. She doubted he could be still for long if he tried. There was such a vibrancy oozing from him that she had never seen in any other man she had met. A pity then that he was unobtainable.

"He could be good for you," Mrs Boyd said gently, disturbing Alice's reverie. "Perhaps it would be worth giving him a chance?"

"I will consider it," Alice answered, not convincing herself or her parents with her words.

Chapter 13

Scotland

The young boy walked into the drawing room, guided and encouraged by his mother, but seeming unsure of the number of people looking at him.

"My word, Cameron! You have grown since the last time I saw you," Lady Kirkbride said, smiling at him. "Come in and make yourself comfortable next to me."

Though he was around eight years old, he was tall for his age and had blonde hair and clear blue eyes. "Thank you, my lady," he said, sitting on the sofa as directed.

"Here are my sons, Hamish and James. My youngest boy is out somewhere, he likes to spend a lot of time on his own, and here is my daughter, Mary, and Lord Kirkbride is there by the fireplace. We have all been eager to meet you."

Cameron looked confused as to why he should have stirred such excitement in so many people, but he tried to smile. Glancing around at the others, Lady Kirkbride saw him swallow, looking very overwhelmed and took pity on him.

"I have ordered you biscuits, but before they arrive you must tell me how your uncle is," she said.

"He wanted me to stay," Cameron said guilelessly. "He was not happy when he received Mama's letter."

"You must be a very good boy if he did not want to be parted from you," Lady Kirkbride encouraged.

"I am. My uncle says I am the best nephew anyone could have."

"Your uncle sounds like a nice man."

"He is. He sent off my tutor, who beat me, and said he will teach me everything I need to know. We are going to start boxing lessons and fencing lessons when I am ten, for he says a gentleman needs to know how to fight."

Constance interrupted before Cameron could say anything else. "Uncle never seeks my approval on anything he does. Lessons can be changed when you return to me."

"But I don't want to!" Cameron exclaimed. "Uncle said I could stay with him forever. It is no fun with you since Da died."

"Your uncle does not know everything. You are to have a new… Oh, I will write to him and sort it out. I will not have my plans disrupted when everything is finally working out how I planned," Constance snapped, almost betraying what she had threatened could not be said. She fumed at her son, and he shrank into Lady Kirkbride's side, who wrapped a protective arm around him.

The room stilled at Constance's words. Hamish and Mary were clearly trying to stop themselves from laughing at what Constance had revealed. James had been staring at Cameron intently since he had come into the room, but Lord and Lady Kirkbride moved to defuse the situation before it could turn into a full-blown argument between mother and son.

"Ah, here are the tea things," Lady Kirkbride said. "I ordered some lemonade for you, Cameron. I hope you like it."

"Oh yes, I eat and drink anything. Uncle says I'd eat two potatoes more than a pig if I was allowed."

Hamish burst out laughing. "I like your uncle."

Cameron smiled up at him. "I do too. He sometimes reminds me of Da, and when I feel sad that I can't see Da anymore, Uncle lets me snuggle up to him and tells me all about when Da was a boy."

"That is very kind of him," Mary said, flashing a worried look at James. "We knew your da too."

"Did you? He was the best Da."

"I am sure he was," Mary responded. "I remember him being very kind to me when I was a young girl."

"He would play soldiers and tell me about his friend who was a brave soldier, but he would get sad then and say sometimes we can make mistakes and upset the people we care about the most. He always told me that I should always treasure my friends. That is why I am good for Uncle; he is my best friend."

James strode to the window and looked blindly outside, a lump in his throat. It was the first time he had heard anything of what Simon had felt about what had happened between them. When James had returned home and found that Constance was married to Simon and had a child, he had raged and beaten Simon. He had seen the look in Simon's eyes, and it was one of sadness, and his friend had not fought back, accepting the beating for his betrayal.

For the first time since it happened, James regretted not being calm enough to have spoken to Simon. It was a chance that was now gone forever, and he was faced with yet another situation he would rather avoid. He inwardly cursed that his life felt out of control, but now was not the time to cause a commotion. For once, he would hold his opinions to himself and act the gentleman he was supposed to be.

"Your da was a good man," James said, surprising everyone.

"I miss him," Cameron said.

"I have some good news that will make you happy," Constance said, glancing at James.

"Not today, Constance," James warned, wondering why she had changed her mind about telling Cameron they were to marry and he was his father.

"But you wanted to tell him…" Constance started, clearly unhappy at being challenged.

"Now is not the time," James growled out. "What is a day or two?"

Constance looked anything but pleased at James commanding her to do as he said, but as she was surrounded by his family, for once, she chose to be magnanimous. "As you wish, but we return on the morrow and then make everything official. I do not think there is any point in delaying."

"I completely agree," James said.

A flicker of something crossed Constance's face, but she soon schooled her features and turned to Cameron. "I think you have eaten enough biscuits for today. We shall leave to stay with Grandmama and return tomorrow."

"Grandmama shouts at me," Cameron whispered to Lady Kirkbride.

"Oh, you poor boy," Lady Kirkbride said. "Perhaps you could remain with us longer tomorrow?"

"Of course. Tomorrow he will be able to stay as long as you wish," Constance said with a pointed look in James's direction.

Goodbyes were said, and after Lady Kirkbride had wrapped the remaining biscuits in a napkin and given them to Cameron, the family were left alone.

Everyone looked towards James, and it was Hamish who broke the silence. "Well, brother?"

"He is the double of Simon!" James exploded. "Any fool could see that I am no more his father than you are."

"Shudder at the thought," Hamish said dramatically.

"She told you he was yours?" Baron Kirkbride asked.

"Yes."

"And you had reason to believe she was telling the truth?"

James squirmed a little under his father's stare. "She claims that I took her innocence on the night before I left, but I was foxed and am ashamed to say I have no memory of anything happening."

"I see, so he could be," Baron Kirkbride said before turning to his wife. "How long have you known that Constance was claiming James was the father?"

Lady Kirkbride blushed at the abrupt way her husband spoke to her. "Constance mentioned it some time ago before she sent the letter; she said she had decided to be honest with James."

"She could not be honest if her life depended on it," Mary snorted.

"And you did not feel able to tell me what she had revealed," the baron continued, ignoring Mary's comment. "We could have perhaps sorted this out before James returned."

"I doubt that very much, Da," James said, coming to the defence of his mother. "Constance has very clear plans that she is intent on seeing through."

"Which involves both you and I dying early, sir," Hamish said with glee. "I do hope she has thought of particularly spectacular demises for us both."

"Hamish!" Lady Kirkbride gasped. "Stop being outrageous."

"I am not guilty on this occasion, Ma. Your future daughter-in-law has to take credit for this scheme. I have been warned to check the stairs for wires when she moves in."

"Interesting that you did not give the same warning to me," Baron Kirkbride said to James with a raised eyebrow.

"I was intending to, Da," James said ruefully. "I did not think you were in danger until she actually lived here."

"Of all the scheming... Well! I do not know what to say," Lady Kirkbride huffed.

"I know exactly what to say," Hamish chipped in. "The boy is Simon's."

"I agree," James said.

"Then you have a way out," Lady Kirkbride said with relief.

"Not when Constance is shouting from the rooftops that James left her with child and abandoned her," Baron Kirkbride said, looking at James. "I hate to admit it, but unless there is something else other than he looks like Simon, we are no better off."

"I know," James said. "I just hate the fact that after everything, she is going to cuckold me, and there is not a damn thing I can do about it. Sorry, Ma. Constance has had the effect of colouring my language since my return."

"Perfectly acceptable in the circumstances," Lady Kirkbride said with a tilt of her head. "It is such a shame, for the boy is a sweetheart, but I still do not wish you to be forced to marry that girl."

"She is hardly a girl," Mary snorted. "She is a calculating witch."

"Mary! There is no need for such talk," Lady Kirkbride scolded.

"James can curse, and everything is fine, yet I speak the truth and I am told off? I think there is not only Constance who has double standards, Ma," Mary said.

Lady Kirkbride laughed at her daughter. "You are right, but it seems worse when a young lady speaks out."

"She is no young lady," Hamish drawled, at which Mary threw a cushion at him.

"Behave, you two! None of this is helping James," Lady Kirkbride said.

Drew chose that moment to walk into the room. "Why does James need help?"

"Because of Constance's scheming," Mary supplied.

"I would keep far away from her, brother, if I were you. She is only concerned for herself, no matter who she walks over," Drew warned.

"Don't I know it," James agreed. "The problem is I have been at fault in some way, and I cannot see a way around it."

"How are you at fault? It was Simon and Constance who lied and misled everyone."

"It sounds as if you know something we are not aware of, brother," Hamish said.

"I do."

"Why the devil have you never brought it up before now?" Hamish asked.

"Leave the boy alone," Baron Kirkbride said. "Tell us what you know, Drew."

"When James left eight years ago, I did not really understand what I had overheard. I understood the words, but not really the implications, that only became apparent when James returned, but because there was so much upset, I did not wish to add to it," Drew said, being serious but without the dramatics which usually followed his speech.

James sat down. "I need to know whatever you have to tell us, but part of me is afraid to hear it."

Drew turned to his older brother. "It might cause you pain, and I am sorry, but hopefully it will help you with Constance after you have heard it."

"Go on," James encouraged.

"The night before you left, you were foxed, and Constance dragged you to the stables," Drew started. No one missed the horrified expression on Lady Kirkbride's face, but Drew continued. "I used to hide in the stables and write in peace, even then. I had been upset when you asked me to help Hamish to look after everyone if you did not return, so I had been there some time trying to control my fear and worry when you and Constance came in."

"Oh Lord!" James muttered to himself.

"Do not worry. You were very jolly about being with Constance, but within minutes you had fallen asleep," Drew said with a smile. "Constance was furious with you, kept pulling at you, slapping your face and shaking you to try and wake you, but you were in a dead sleep, snoring loudly. I had never heard some of the words she used when she was cursing you."

"Nothing happened between us?" James asked, looking up, for the first time a glimmer of hope in his eyes.

"No. Constance continued to curse you and accuse you of not even being sober enough to kiss her, and I thought she would go away and leave you be, but then Simon came in," Drew continued. "Constance started ranting at him, saying trust you to spoil their plans and cause a problem, but Simon was angrier than I had ever seen him. He was saying that they should be honest with you and admit what they had done, that it had been a mistake and for them to beg your forgiveness."

"They had betrayed me before I left?" James asked. Everyone had seen the colour fade from his face as the realisation of what had happened sank in.

"Constance started screaming at Simon, saying if he wanted them to be murdered by you, then he could say what he wished, but she would deny everything. She was going to say that the baby was yours. You were too drunk to know that nothing had happened and that you would believe her over Simon every time. She was gleeful when she said that Simon would lose everything if he opened his mouth to tell the truth."

"The absolute witch – and no, I am not apologising for my use of language, Ma," Mary said.

"For once, Mary, I am in complete agreement with you," Lady Kirkbride said.

"Simon was really unhappy, and he begged her to marry him, wanting to be a father to his child.

Constance made him suffer before she agreed, baiting him that she would marry you and he would never see his son. One thing is certain, Simon did not sound like a man in love, more like a man about to go to the gallows when she finally said that she would marry him," Drew said. "When nothing happened the morning you left, I thought it best to remain silent, and I did not really understand all of what had been said. It is only since becoming a man that I have fully appreciated the implications of their actions."

"Oh, Drew, you never disappoint!" Hamish said with a grin at the final words. "This certainly puts a different light on what your soon-to-be betrothed has been tormenting you with. Are you going to commit murder now? I am sure she will not be missed in the locality; in fact, you would be doing the area a good deed."

"No one is murdering anyone, no matter what they have done," Lady Kirkbride said. "But you are free, James! She cannot threaten you with anything, we all know the truth, and although I have been friends with her mother for years and I am sorry for Simon's family, I will not stand by and watch my son's honour be besmirched in such a way."

"Thank you, Ma," James said, smiling at his mother. "And thank you, Drew. Although I have to say I wish you had mentioned something a few days ago, I would certainly have slept better."

"I did not know what Constance was intending to do until today," Drew answered. "You probably would not have believed me if I would have said anything. In the past, you would never allow anyone to have a bad word said against her."

"True, but I was blinded with infatuation," James said.

"Which is why I shall never marry," Hamish drawled. "It makes one lose sense or even worse be managed by a termagant."

"It looks like the continuation of the family name is down to you, Drew," Baron Kirkbride said to much laughter at Drew's expression of horror. "What are you going to do, James?"

"I am going to speak to Constance. And it is not going to be pretty."

Chapter 14

London

It was abundantly clear that Mr Mortimer was trying to gain the affection of Alice. Everyone could see it, even Alice, which made meetings with him distinctly uncomfortable.

"Archie, please accompany me," she pleaded to her brother when needing to visit the publisher.

"I would only be in the way. Take a maid, you do not need me anymore; Mortimer has your best interests at heart," Archie replied.

"But you being there would make sure it is only inane topics that we speak about. If you do not attend with me, he will start to spout speeches that I really do not wish to hear."

"I do not understand you sometimes, Alice," Archie said, shaking his head at his sister. "Anyone else in your position would be delighted with the way your life has turned out, yet you constantly seem unhappy. Surely this cannot still be about that Scot who turned your head?"

"He did not just turn my head! It was far more than that and you know it. I despair of you; there is not a single romantic bone in your body," Alice cursed her brother.

"You say that as if it is a problem. You are the romantic one in the family, whereas I am more business-minded, hence I managed to negotiate a good deal for you. I did not realise at the time that I was also finding a husband for you."

"I like Mr Mortimer as my publisher, nothing more."

Archie became serious. "Alice, you need to think long and hard before you dismiss Mortimer as a husband. I know we are not poor, but we do not have a never-ending supply of money either. The estate is small, and although profitable, it is not bringing in riches. I know you are earning money with your books, but how long will that last? Have you three books in you, six, twenty-six? And will publishers want them all? We both know how fashions change. I promise to support you after our mother and father are gone if you remain unwed, but a husband and marriage would provide a more secure future for you."

"I feel like a donkey being sold to anyone who will have her," Alice muttered.

"Not at all, Mortimer is besotted. I would not encourage you to marry someone who I did not think would treat you well," Archie said. "I know he has your best interests at heart, and if you marry, he will be doubly motivated to make sure you are a success."

"I do not need to marry anyone. I did not expect to. After all, I am six and twenty and have managed to escape it so far."

"You sound like a man and not like your usual romantic self." Archie laughed. "Do not try to convince me that you do not wish to be married. All women want to be wed."

"To sit around talking, doing needlework and having child after child until you are fit to do nothing? No thank you! I do not find that future at all tempting."

"But if your Highlander proposed?" Archie asked. "Would this new opinion on marriage suddenly change?"

Alice decided it was not time to admit that James had suggested they marry, and it was she who had told him she wanted a more romantic proposal. She now felt a complete fool for uttering those words. If she had accepted him and they had got a special licence, she would be wed and happily doing any amount of needlework that was required. "He will not, so there is no point asking about something that is not going to happen," she said stiffly, unable to hide the hurt she was constantly struggling to dampen down every time she thought of what could have been. "I suppose I had better accept that I need to ask a maid to accompany me as you are determined to be disobliging."

"Oh, do not look at me in that way," Archie groaned. "You are a spoiled little sister."

"Does that mean you will not abandon me?" she asked hopefully.

"Order the carriage. I will be ready in half an hour."

Alice flung her arms around her brother's neck. "Thank you! I will dedicate my next book to you."

"I should hope so. It is pitiful watching a man mooning over someone who could not care less about him."

"I could never be so callous. I like him, but there could never be anything else other than fondness for him."

"Many marriages have started with less," Archie said. "Fine! I am going, don't glare daggers at me. I pity the man who does eventually marry you."

As the pair left the morning room and Alice ordered the carriage to be brought round, she felt real relief that Archie had agreed to accompany her. Mr Mortimer was becoming very persistent, and seeing him was increasingly uncomfortable. She would not admit it to her family, for they would just presume, rightly, that she was still longing for James, but it was more than that. Not one to hide from the person who was selling a lot of books and keen to sell more, she was determined that every meeting would be on her terms, preventing a renewal of Mr Mortimer's protestations of affection.

As they were about to leave, Frances, another member of the Bluestocking Club, arrived to see Alice.

"Please join us," Alice said when Frances started to apologise for her poor timing. "We can visit Serena afterwards."

"Are you sure?" Frances asked.

"Most certainly, for you can be chaperone on this outing, rather than I," Archie said.

"Oh no! You can still accompany us to Mr Mortimer's, and then we will drop you off wherever you would like," Alice said.

"That is very generous of you."

"I thought so."

***

On entering Serena's house, the two friends were still chatting about Mr Mortimer as Serena greeted them.

"What have I missed?" Serena asked.

"Mr Mortimer has hinted that unless certain criteria are met, they might not consider publishing any of Alice's work after the first three books," Frances explained.

"Really? But they have already ordered another print run! Every time I have seen him, he is waxing lyrical about how well sales are. Is this to do with your reluctance around him, Alice?" Serena asked.

"I am afraid it is, but I am so glad I begged Archie to go with me. He absolutely roasted Mr Mortimer and threatened that he would immediately start to look for a publisher who had good business sense and was not ruled by foolish romantic notions," Alice said.

"Oh dear. I am surprised you aren't still blushing, it must have been very embarrassing," Serena said.

"It was. I do not think I was ever more mortified, not helped by the fact I could see my publishing career ending almost before it has started."

"Your brother is right, though, any publisher would snap you up with the way things have gone. I think Mr Mortimer will regret threatening you."

"I think he was wishing he had not spoken, almost from the moment Archie started taking him to task over his thinly veiled threats," Frances said with glee. "Archie was very forceful and eloquent."

"For once." Alice grinned. "It seems his years of practice with his set-downs to the younger generations of fops and the like has set him in good stead for putting businessmen in place. I do not think he will be quite so encouraging when trying to persuade me to marry Mr Mortimer in future."

"Why has he been encouraging you to do that?" Frances asked.

"Because it will give me security," Alice sighed. "Which it would, but I am loath to accept that as the only reason for marriage."

"Especially when a certain captain is still in your heart," Serena said gently.

Alice looked at her friend, pain in her expression. "I wish every day that he was not. He is probably married by now and playing happy families with that woman."

"I doubt that would ever happen," Serena said. "I feel heartily sorry for anyone unfortunate enough to be married to her. I have never met someone so unpleasant in my life."

"You have been out of the London season for a while," Frances said. "It seems the Bluestockings are a target for ridicule this year, they forget we have two titled ladies in our ranks, but it seems when they are not with us, we are a bunch of dreary spinsters who are pretending to be intelligent."

"Of all the... Oh, the narrow-mindedness of people!" Serena huffed. "Who has said that?"

"There is a group of debutantes, and I think they feel threatened by women who refuse to speak only of muslin and the latest on-dit. It is almost funny to think that in reality we are no threat to them, the men dislike our conversation just as much as they do," Frances said.

"We have chosen not to marry," Serena said to Frances. "It is not through want of beaus; it is just they would have bored us within a sennight, let alone the rest of our lives."

"I know, and I do agree, but do you not think that sometimes, just once or twice, it would be nice to feel normal?" Frances said.

"You are normal! It is those girls who are ridiculous," Alice defended her friend and her other Bluestocking friends.

"I am seven and twenty with not a single proposal that I can boast about because every time I start to speak about the benefit of certain plants for health, I see the glazing over of their eyes. Either that or they think I am some sort of witch. I understand that if I really do wish to be what everyone considers acceptable, I would need to give up on my plants, and I just cannot do that."

"You are perfect and so knowledgeable that you must not change, but I do wish you were a witch, we could have so much fun. You could magic holes in dresses at the most inappropriate times and hair to fall out of its clips," Alice laughed. She understood completely what Frances felt as she, too, had wished to be normal over the years. Frances was fun to be around and handsome rather than pretty, but had such charm and grace about her that Alice often wondered why someone could not see her value as her friends could.

"I would more likely be burned at the stake," Frances replied dryly.

"Do not joke about that," Serena shuddered. "In an effort to turn our minds away from all things witchy, I would like your permission to send Mary the three volumes of your book, Alice. I have already bought a set, and I admit that I was going to just send them to her, but then I felt uncomfortable doing it without your knowledge. Would you mind? I know she would love to read it."

Alice sighed, all silliness gone. "The reality is that he will be living somewhere else with his new family now, so sending them to Mary would in no way bring me to his attention. You can send them with my blessing and the hope that she gets some pleasure from them."

"Thank you. I will parcel them up later," Serena said. "Now I think it is time we forgot all about foolish men and silly debutantes and ask all about the luncheon with the patronesses."

"Oh lord! You had to bring that up, didn't you?" Alice groaned.

"It is only two days off, and I was hoping that when they give you a voucher for Almack's, they include Frances and I in the invitation, as there are only us three left in town at the moment."

"I wish I could be out of town," Alice said. "If they do not include you two in the voucher, there is no point my going, whether it is Almack's or not, for I would be lost without some of my Bluestockings by my side."

"We will be there because I am sure you will amaze the patronesses at their luncheon as you do us," Frances said.

***

"That was most interesting," Lady Jersey said after Alice had come to the end of her reading.

Alice was not sure that she meant the words, but she accepted them with good grace. One did not upset the group of ladies she was with, or there was no point in staying in London, for they could make a person, and they could certainly break someone if they chose to.

"How do you find the time to write? I hardly have time to go through my invitations, let alone attend events. I barely write letters during the season, let alone three volumes of a novel," Lady Jersey continued. "And why did you put your name on the book? Would it not be better to have remained anonymous like other ladies who write?"

"Come now, Sally," Lady Sefton scolded. "You can see the poor girl is terrified of you. Stop bullying her."

"I was just asking reasonable questions," Sally Jersey sniffed at her friend before turning back to Alice. "You have done well; everyone is talking about your book. I have it on my bedside table to read."

"Thank you, my lady. I hope it does not disappoint," Alice said.

"I hope so too."

Lady Sefton smiled at Alice. "She has already read the first two volumes and is considering missing a ball tonight in order that she might finish it," she said as the formidable Lady Jersey moved to speak to one of her other friends. "If it ends the way she wants it to, you can guarantee huge sales as she will browbeat everyone she knows into buying copies."

"Oh dear, I am not sure what would be worse, her hating it or loving it," Alice grimaced.

Lady Sefton laughed. "I completely understand your feeling, but I cannot imagine she will be disappointed, she has talked of little else, which is why I was so pleased you had already agreed to join us when she started reading it."

"It was a great privilege to attend, and I can only thank you again for allowing me to have the opportunity," Alice said with genuine gratitude. "I might be terrified, but I am not unaware of the honour it is to be here."

Patting Alice's hand, Lady Sefton smiled at her. "You will go far, my dear, I am sure of it, and it might start with meeting some handsome gentleman at Almack's. I will introduce you to anyone I think would be a suitable match. You are not the only one who likes happy endings."

Lady Cowper overheard what Lady Sefton had said and leaned over to speak. "I do too. Shall we make Miss Boyd our pet project?" she asked her friend.

"What schemes are you thinking of?" Lady Sefton asked with a laugh at the gregarious woman; it was typical of her to think of something outrageous to do.

"Let us make sure she is the diamond of the season," Lady Cowper said.

"But I am too old!" Alice exclaimed, her shock at what was being suggested betraying her into speaking.

Lady Cowper laughed. "You are younger than I."

"By a couple of years, that is all," Alice said.

"And that is why you should be the hit of the season," Lady Cowper said. "Show these young things that there is life after they turn twenty."

"We do not want to encourage her to follow your example," Lady Sefton said with a raised eyebrow at her friend.

"Oh pfft!" Lady Cowper said. "I am determined to enjoy my life."

"And you certainly do."

It was clear that Lady Sefton was referring to things that Alice knew nothing about, and she certainly did not wish to know if Lady Cowper's chuckle was any indication. Alice might be intelligent about the ways of the world, but she was also technically an innocent and feeling completely out of her depth.

"We shall promote you to all the right people, and you will have everyone knocking on your door before too long, wanting to see more of the delightful Miss Boyd. Especially if we suggest that your book is based on some of the members of the *ton*," Lady Cowper said mischievously.

There was nothing Alice could say in response, so she smiled and hoped that the panic she had felt at Lady Cowper's words was not visible. To be introduced to gentlemen by one of the patronesses was a terrifying thought, but to have them suggesting that she had written about her peers was a recipe for disaster. They could do as they pleased, but her reputation and good name could not take a scandal.

Sighing to herself, she sipped her tea and wondered where the giant of a Scot was when he was needed to laugh her out of her worry. She would be able to distract herself if she could torment and tease him. In fact, she would not be in this predicament if he was near; he would protect her from anyone determined to cause mischief. She ached at the fact she would never see him again, see the glower he aimed in everyone's direction at some point and the way his eyes softened when he looked at her.

Heart feeling heavy, she hoped he was happy. That way, at least one of them was.

Chapter 15

Scotland

"He is Simon's son!" James roared at Constance the moment they were left alone. Lady Kirkbride had acted quickly when Constance and Cameron had arrived, hurrying the boy away from his mother with the promise that Mary was waiting for him in the stables and Cook had made cake.

"He is yours!" Constance snapped in return. "You cannot avoid the connection. I will not let you abandon him and cast him off!"

"You know damn well that I would never abandon a child of mine, and that is what you were relying on, was it not? That my misplaced sense of loyalty would support you though you have done nothing to earn my good opinion."

Constance's eyes were flashing, but James could see that she was trying to rein in her temper. "You once told me you would love me forever." Her tone was gentle, almost wistful.

"That was the infatuation of a man who knew no better," James snapped.

"You can be the most horrible person I have ever met. I made one mistake. Am I always to be punished for it?"

"One mistake?" James ground out, gritting his teeth. "I think you have memory problems if that is what you consider the truth of the matter."

"We laid together, James; it was wonderful. Please. We can recreate those feelings, I am sure of it. For Cameron's sake, if for nothing else."

"It was wonderful, was it?" James snarled.

"We both wanted it to happen. I was so afraid that you would find someone else, and then your letters were so irregular that I panicked, and Simon offered to support me so I would not be ruined."

"Convenient."

"I was in an impossible situation!" Constance snapped, reverting to her usual habit of making herself out to be the victim in every situation.

"Yes, you were," James said.

Stepping towards him, Constance touched his arm, but he shook her off. "James, he is yours."

"I do not know how you can say that when we did not lay with each other. I was too foxed to do anything, and you cursed like the devil when I fell asleep."

Momentarily stunned, Constance opened her mouth and then, recollecting herself, she crossed her arms. "That would be a perfect excuse for you to abandon us if it were true."

"We both know it is; we were seen and overheard."

"That is very fortuitous, is it not?" Constance laughed. "Someone overheard us! Tell me, was it Hamish or Mary? They would say anything to disoblige me by making me out the liar and protect you."

"It was neither of them," James responded coolly.

"You expect me to believe that? They treat me like a fool, but I hear their mutterings, and I am fully aware of their opinion of me. Who else would it be?"

"Why should their opinion of you be of any concern? You are planning Hamish's demise so that you can be Lady Kirkbride." James laughed bitterly.

"I am thinking of Cameron. He would thrive with a title to open up opportunities that he would not have, and let us be honest, Hamish is hardly a good representation of how a titled gentleman should be."

"Damn you, woman, why can't you see what the boy has already? Let him go back to his uncle. It is obvious they dote on each other, and he is to inherit, that would be the best for the boy. He is clearly happy with his uncle." James was sick of the argument and what felt like going round in circles. It was another indication that he had not really known Constance before he left, either that or he was infatuated enough to have ignored her true character.

"It is not better for me!" Constance snapped. "I remain the widow who let down the town hero, looked at with derision and contempt. I am sick of it."

"You should have thought about that before you married Simon."

"I have explained my reasonings."

James rubbed a hand through his hair. "Constance, in God's name, be honest for once. You laid with Simon before I left. You were already increasing, and your attempt to bed me was to hurry a wedding whilst saving your reputation. You mistimed it. I went away before you could force me into marriage, but you betrayed me before I left, nothing to do with my being away or not keeping in touch. Simon wanted to confess all, and it was you who stopped him."

Constance's colour drained from her face and she seemed at a loss. Eventually, she whispered, "When did you find out? Did you know before you left?"

"No. If I had, I would probably have got myself killed purposely," James said.

"I do not understand how you found out. No one knew," Constance insisted, the fight gone out of her for the moment at least.

"I spoke the truth when I said that you were overheard after I had fallen asleep and Simon came to the stables. I wish I had known that you were not happy with me, although I suppose you have never really been content, have you? All your scheming for your advancement has shown me that. You were prepared to cast off everything you had shared with Simon and erase his memory in order to get what you considered a bigger prize. You probably even failed to recognise you had secured a good man in Simon while he was alive."

"He never could truly love me," Constance said, finally being candid but biting out the words in anger.

"The guilt of betraying your friendship ate at him, the fool. He could never forgive himself or me. I wanted a house full of children, but he barely came near me and never after you returned home. You destroyed any chance I had at happiness."

"I think you did that yourself," James mocked her. "You managed to sever any ties I had with a man I considered a brother. Excuse me for not feeling upset that it did not work out between the two of you."

"He wanted what you had!" Constance snapped. "He chased me, not the other way around."

"I find that hard to believe, but it does not matter, he is gone, and we can never find out the truth."

"I am sure he died in part to spite me. He loved Cameron, but I think he had lost the will to live after seeing you. When he became ill, he saw it as a way to stop his pain, not considering how Cameron or I would manage without his support."

"Do you know how selfish that sounds?" James asked incredulously.

Constance touched James's arm. "I thought I had everything, but then I lost the love of you both. It is not too late for us, James. We can make it work for our sakes and Cameron. Think of it as caring for Simon's son if nothing else. I know he would rest in peace if he knew it was you taking care of us."

James shook off her hand and moved away from her. "I cannot believe what gall you have! There is nothing you would not do to achieve what you want, is there? And yet the answer is staring you in the face."

"Yes, marry you."

"Never. You have the opportunity of doing the best by your son. Let him go back to his uncle. Why don't you join them? Being away from this town might do you the world of good." James had finished being upset by what had happened in the past. He could not believe how wrong he had been about Constance and felt immeasurable relief that he was no longer being forced into a marriage with her.

"That would certainly suit your family," Constance said dryly. "And it would enable you to chase that bookish woman who pitifully followed you."

"Nothing that woman does is pitiful," James responded.

"You are going to marry her."

"No, I am not. She would not have me."

"Then she is a fool," Constance snorted. "If you change your mind about us, I will be with Cameron's uncle. I will collect Cameron and return with him. I know I am not welcome there, but he will put up with my demands if it means he has Cameron with him."

"Can you not just be nice for once? Do not demand, ask."

"And be told no? I am not that foolish. If I do not have the upper hand, then there is a chance I will lose everything. Cameron is my only bargaining tool."

"Then I am sorry for you but more so for the boy."

"You lost the right to have an opinion on my parenting skills when you refused to marry me," Constance snapped.

"That I did. I wish you well," James said, meaning the words. "But I hope Cameron grows up always in touch with his uncle."

"For he would not fare well purely from my influence, is that what you are trying to say?" James shrugged, and for the first time Constance laughed. "I do not deserve him, but luckily for me, he takes after his father and not his mother. Goodbye, James, I did love you, you know. I realise I had a strange way of showing it, but at the start, I truly loved you."

"It no longer matters what either of us felt."

"I just wanted you to know it was not all false."

James nodded once, and Constance walked out of the room. Walking over to the window, James stared out unseeing into the gardens of the home he had loved and still did, but there was something missing, and it caused an ache deep inside.

He had lost her, and he did not think he would ever recover.

Not turning when the door opened, he looked over his shoulder when his father greeted him. "Constance seemed resigned when she left. I am hoping that means you are not being forced to do as she wished after all?" Baron Kirkbride asked.

"No. Thank God Drew overheard the conversation and was old enough to remember it," James replied.

"Are we to lose you to London now? I expect Miss Boyd will also be happy at the outcome of this fiasco."

James laughed bitterly. “She is a good enough person that she would be glad for me, but she was very clear even before I returned home that she would never accept second best. Even if I begged for another chance, there would be no hope.”

“I am sorry to hear that. Perhaps you can convince her that she never was second best,” Baron Kirkbride said gently.

James looked at his father. “You really miss nothing, do you? How did Hamish and I ever get away with anything when we were younger?”

“Oh, boys should be allowed a certain amount of freedom as they grow. I must admit your mother was not too happy about my allowing you to run wild over the estate, but I assured her you would not come to any harm.”

“Hamish might disagree, the way he moaned for months over his broken arm,” James chuckled.

“It was character building.” The baron smiled. “Although my ears suffered from your mother’s cursings as a result of the accident.”

“Now that is something that I wish I had heard.” James sighed. “I am at a loss, Pa. What do I do now there is no war? I feel as if I have no purpose.”

“Take your time. Rest,” the baron said. “These last years have seen you facing things most would never wish to see, and then you had the betrayal to face. You will find your role in the world. If not, you could always go into the clergy.” The baron’s words caused the genuine laugh he hoped it would, and he patted his son on the shoulder. "Be easy, son. Things will turn out for the best."

***

A few days later, Mary burst into the morning room, holding a parcel and an open letter in her hand. "Look! Miss Boyd's book!"

James looked up sharply. "She has sent you copies?"

"No. They have been sent by Serena," Mary replied. "She says Alice is aware that she sent the parcel and sends her best wishes and hopes that I enjoy the novel. How grand do the volumes look? Can we choose a good binding, Ma? I am sure this is a book we will be returning to time and again."

"Of course. I hope you will start to read it to us this evening. We should enjoy it together," Lady Kirkbride said. "Let us see if there is anyone we recognise in the story."

James snorted. "I asked something similar once, and the cheeky lassie said I was not interesting enough to appear in a novel."

"She knew you well then," Hamish drawled.

James mock-glared at his brother, but Mary interrupted any further taunts. "Listen to what Serena says...

> *Alice is quite the celebrity in town. The Almack's patronesses have decided that she is their pet project, and*

she has been introduced to everyone of importance. There is talk that the Prince Regent wishes to meet her, but Alice is terrified she will upset him, mainly because the rogue in her story is loosely based on him.

Her face when Lady Jersey said that the Regent was keen to make her acquaintance was hilarious to see, but we will ensure she is not alone in that meeting, for it is more likely that the Regent has heard how popular Alice has become and wants to chase her himself.

Honestly, her home is full of flowers from her admirers, and she never sits down now at balls, her hand is constantly sought. If I am being truthful, I think she is overwhelmed by the attention, which was caused by her publisher insisting she needed to publish under her own name and give talks. It seems his method was sound in the business sense because they can hardly keep up with demand. I confess the publisher is also smitten with Alice, but who wouldn't be? She is so good with everyone who is vying for her attention, and I am so happy to see her receive the recognition she deserves. There is almost a queue of gentlemen when morning calls begin. I am so glad she is such a success. Even without the patronesses' support, she was being well received, but this is something she was not expecting.

I hope you are all well and happy. One day you must come to London, do it soon because the gentlemen who lose out to dancing with Alice seek out her friends. It is good fun and very entertaining. Honestly, we never stop laughing! With best wishes, Serena."

"I am so glad she has been successful," Lady Kirkbride said. "She is such a lovely girl."

"Sounds to me like she needs some sort of protector." Hamish gave his brother a pointed look.

"To keep her away from men who can provide her very own romantic gestures?" James asked. "No. She is getting the success she deserves, and I am happy for her."

"If you could say that without the sad, haunted eyes, it might be more convincing. Possibly." Hamish laughed at his brother's discomfort. "I never had you down as a defeatist."

"I am not. I am a realist. You should try it sometime."

"No, thank you. It seems so drearily boring. Ma, I hope you can talk some sense into him, for I give up. I cannot deal with someone who is lost in a puddle of self-pity."

"Not a pool?" Mary asked.

"No. That would be far too dramatic, even for our rejected suitor," Hamish said, leaving the room.

"I hate to admit it because when he is right it makes him insufferable," Mary started. "But he is right.

I think you need to go to Alice and make a grand gesture."

James snorted. "And make a complete fool of myself? No. I am staying here. If she wants me, she knows where to find me."

"That is the most foolish comment I have ever heard you utter," Lady Kirkbride said, surprising her son with her sharp tone. "How on earth could she visit here, thinking you are married to Constance? Idiotish boy!"

"I could write to Serena?" Mary offered.

"No!" James shot out. "Leave her be, she deserves better than me, and by the sounds of it, she is going to have the choice of her circle. I wish her well, but do not interfere, Mary, it will not end well."

"Fine!" Mary said, struggling to hold her hands up in defeat whilst carrying the three volumes of the novel and the letter. "For once, I agree with Hamish. You are wallowing, and it is not an attractive trait."

"Even more reason she would not want me," James said, leaving the room.

Mary and Lady Kirkbride were left staring at each other in dismay.

"He will come around, surely?" Mary asked. "They are perfect for each other."

"I hope so, for I cannot imagine Alice is enjoying the fuss as much as Serena implies. She did not like being the centre of attention, that much was clear. I can only imagine what all the furore is doing to her."

"You never know; she might be enjoying herself," Mary said doubtfully.

"For her sake, I hope she is, because it seems your foolish brother is not going to do anything to help them both."

"Poor Alice."

"Yes, indeed."

Chapter 16

London

"I hate this!" Alice ground out when surrounded by her Bluestocking friends. "I wish Grace was here to ask her advice. She would know how to get out of this without losing face."

"It is everything you have ever wanted," Frances pointed out.

"Which makes me the most ungrateful chit, does it not?" Alice sighed. "It is just being the plaything of the patronesses; it is in equal parts terrifying and – just terrifying!"

"Could you perhaps explain to Lady Sefton? She seems approachable, more so than the others at least," Serena suggested.

"And risk them turning against me? I might not have minded being on the edges of society, but that does not mean I wish to be permanently excluded," Alice said. "It is silly. A year ago, I would have probably loved every moment of what has happened."

"But that was before a handsome Scot stole your heart," Serena said gently. It was not a question, everyone knew that Alice was still repining over her lost love.

"Yes, more fool me," Alice said. "I wish I could shake off this melancholy, I really do. I hate myself for this is not who I am."

"You really are too hard on yourself," Frances assured her. "Grace would definitely tell you to allow yourself time to heal."

"I suspect that she would be speaking from experience," Alice said in agreement. "I often wonder who it was who broke Grace's heart."

"She could have broken his," Serena offered.

"No. I recognise that look of longing." Alice smiled at her friend. "I hope after all the years have passed, she is still not waking up thinking of him nor going to sleep thinking of him."

"That sounds like bitter experience speaking," Serena said.

"Oh yes."

"You need something to take your mind off him," Frances said firmly.

"If the balls, parties and theatre trips have not had an impact, I doubt anything else will stop her pain," Serena said. "I am sure you have lost weight these last weeks."

"I certainly have. My dancing shoes need replacing. I have worn them for the last three years, hardly used, but this year, let me just say I will not need to wear them soon, the soles are so thin," Alice laughed.

"In that case, I think we need a shopping expedition," Frances said eagerly. "And if we can call at the circulating library on the way home, even better."

Alice looked at Serena. "She knows there is a new book out on plants, doesn't she?"

Serena nodded. "Definitely, or she would never have agreed to go shopping so eagerly. Resign yourself to spending an hour in the library."

"I know which book I want!" Frances exclaimed.

"And then something else will catch your eye, and then you will have to check the other authors, just in case," Alice said. "I could have written a novel before we can drag you out."

"That is a good thing since your publisher is demanding the second book from you," Frances said.

Alice groaned. "Yes, and no matter what I try, the words are not flowing."

"No wonder with all the entertainments," Serena said. "I am surprised you can even think of a story."

"True enough." Alice knew it was not completely to do with how busy she was. It certainly was having an impact on the time she had to write, but the real problem was whenever she sat, and there were no other intrusions, all she could think about was James; wondering what he was doing and if he was happy.

Knowing she had to find a way of stopping thoughts of him was easier than putting it into practice.

***

Returning from a successful shopping trip, Alice felt lighter than she had in a while. Grateful for her friends who had her best interests at heart, she entered the house humming.

Surprised to see her father in the hallway rather than a footman, she was immediately on the alert. "What is it, Papa?" she asked, putting down the few parcels which held her purchases.

"Your mother is entertaining Mr Mortimer. He has been waiting for you for the last half hour," Mr Boyd said.

"Oh, really? Is Archie available to join me? I would not like any discussions about the next book without him being there," Alice said, removing her gloves and bonnet as she spoke.

"This time Archie is unnecessary. My love, he has asked for my permission to ask you to marry him."

"Oh." Alice sat heavily in a chair. "You have not refused him permission, have you?" she asked with hope.

"I considered it but then thought we were all doing him a disservice," Mr Boyd said. "I would never force you into a marriage you did not wish for, but he has been consistently attentive, and I think it only fair that he is given a chance to plead his case. If you then refuse him, he will go away knowing that he did his best. And you never know, you might decide that what he offers is what you want."

"Because this is probably the last proposal I will get?"

"I want you to be happy, that is all. If you decide to remain unmarried, that is perfectly acceptable to me. All I ask is that you listen to a man who seems besotted."

Alice grimaced. "That is going to make the refusal all the more difficult."

"Now, now, I would expect more of you than to be so dismissive of a person's feelings," Mr Boyd chastised.

"I am sorry, Papa. I think this being a pet of the patronesses has gone to my head," Alice said, standing and kissing her father's cheek. "I will listen and I will be kind."

"You are a good girl, your mother and I just want you to be happy."

"And that is why you are the best of parents," Alice said, moving towards the drawing room. She dreaded what conversation would have to take place, but her father was correct when he said Mr Mortimer deserved a hearing. "Good afternoon, Mr Mortimer."

Mrs Boyd stood the moment her daughter entered. "Alice! You have finally returned. Was it a successful trip?"

"It was, thank you. My apologies, Mr Mortimer. I did not expect a visit from you or I would most certainly have returned earlier."

"I decided to visit at the last moment," Mr Mortimer bowed to Alice, sitting when she did.

"If you will excuse me, I need to speak to Cook about something," Mrs Boyd said. "I will leave the door open, just a little."

Alice flushed at her mother's obvious words and looked down. She was gripping her hands together as if facing something unpleasant, and she forced herself to try and relax. "I want to assure you that I am not out every day shopping, I do try to write often," she said, hoping to keep the mood light. "Perhaps not as often as my publisher would like, but I hope not to disappoint."

"You could never do anything other than charm me, Miss Boyd," Mr Mortimer said, betraying his nerves by gripping his gloves tightly.

Alice was struck that he had kept hold of his gloves instead of leaving them with his hat and cane. She felt sorry for him, for he was about to propose to someone who had been clearly rebuffing his attempts at being romantic. "You are too kind," she said.

"Miss Boyd, it is no good, I know you do not feel for me as I do for you, and I admit that trying to threaten you with no further publication was a despicable thing to do, but I was at a loss as to how I could persuade you to marry me." The words were said in a rush, high colour on his cheeks and his brow looking shiny.

"I…" Alice started.

"Please," he said, interrupting her. "Let me say this, and then if you refuse me, I will utter not another word on the subject, but be assured that I will always protect your business interests. I am now man enough to be able to separate the two."

Alice nodded slightly, there was no point in trying to speak again; he had clearly built himself into a frenzy of words which needed to be said.

"I promise that if you marry me, I will love and care for you until my dying day. I am a wealthy man. I know that sounds as if I think you are bothered by such, but if I could not provide you with a good home and income, believe me, I would not offer. I have spoken to your father about my finances and he seemed surprised, but I have invested wisely, kept my living costs down, until now, and have planned for a good life when I eventually found my life-mate. I am a businessman and hope you can overlook that. I wish there was something I could do that would not result in some of your circle being disparaging about the fact, but I promise to make up for that in every way I can."

"Mr Boyd, you are sounding like you are describing a prize bull with the way you are listing everything about yourself. Please be at ease," Alice pleaded.

Sagging into the chair, he smiled at her ruefully. "I am making a hash of this, am I not? I knew I would."

Alice looked at him, really looked. He was dressed in the finest clothes any member of the *ton* would be happy to be seen in. He might have saved every penny he could, but he obviously liked to be well turned out. His face was attractive, not as handsome as – but she was being unfair in comparing him to what she considered perfection. And someone who was unobtainable, she must not forget that.

"I know what you are asking, and I hate that it was causing you discomfort," Alice said.

"Only because I know how I will feel if I fail in my quest."

"You have been very kind to me, apart from when you went a little foolish," she said of the thinly veiled threats he had issued.

"I wish I could go back in time and have that conversation again. I was a fool, and I am so sorry and ashamed that I even thought about it, never mind that I actually uttered the words."

"Do not concern yourself, I am teasing you. I think you came off worst after my brother was done berating you."

Mr Mortimer chuckled. "There was certainly no doubt about his feelings on the matter," he said. "It did me good to be roasted by him; it brought me to my senses."

Alice was relieved that he was more relaxed, that was until her father walked into the room. "Papa, is there anything amiss?" Alice said, both herself and Mr Mortimer standing at Mr Boyd's entrance.

"I am so sorry to barge in," Mr Boyd glanced in sympathy at Mr Mortimer. "But an express has arrived for you from Lydia, and the boy is saying he has to return with an answer."

"Lydia? Whatever can have happened?" Tearing the seal off the letter, she quickly skimmed the hastily written missive and looked up at her father. "There is a problem. She needs me."

"Is she ill?" Mr Boyd asked.

"She has not specified exactly, but she urges me to come as soon as I can. Please let me write a short reply." Moving to the table, she wrote quickly and handed the note to her father.

"You are going?" Mr Boyd asked.

"Of course, Lydia never would ask for help unless it was important. You know how independent she has always been," she said of the friend who had spent a lot of the time with Alice's family to avoid her own difficult parents.

"That is true. I will send this off. My apologies again," Mr Boyd said to Mr Mortimer.

Silence fell when Mr Boyd had left the room. Mr Mortimer had remained standing. "It seems my timing could have been better," he said ruefully. "Are you really leaving at this point in the season? Even I know how people can fall out of favour if they are not constantly in the middle of everything."

"Worried about sales?" Alice smiled at him.

"No! Not at all," Mr Mortimer said. "I just presumed that you were enjoying the social whirl you have been swept up in."

Alice gave a non-committal sound, but his words had proved to her once again how unmatched they were. He did not know her, and she was not sure she wanted him to.

As if reading her thoughts, he took a step towards her. "Miss Boyd, Alice, you know what I want, even through my bumbling, I think you understood that I was determined to propose to you today. I know your thoughts will already be with your friend, but could I ask one thing of you?"

"Of course." Alice appreciated that he was not about to continue the uncomfortable conversation.

"Please think over my proposal while you are away. I will not contact you unless I have to, but please seriously consider what I am offering. That is all I ask. I promise that I will spend my life trying to make you happy if you accept, and you never know, one day you might love me, just a little."

"Mr Mortimer, I do not deserve your love. No one should marry a person who does not love them."

"Do not worry, I am once more being realistic. I am happy that you like me; for now, that will make me content, I assure you."

Bowing over her hand, he took his leave, and Alice slumped into a chair with a whoosh of breath. "Alice, you are a bigger fool than anyone you know," she muttered to herself. "You have a man who professes to adore you, and yet you insist on pining after someone who is married to another. You deserve to be locked away."

"What was that, Alice?" Mrs Boyd said, entering the room. "Your father has told me about Lydia's letter."

"I was just wondering when would be the best time to set out," Alice lied.

"I will help you pack. Will you be taking Serena with you?"

"No. I will just take Betsey with me," she said of her maid. "It is not fair to drag Serena away for a second time. I will need to send letters to her and Frances. I just hope Lydia is well."

"I am sure there is nothing to worry about," Mrs Boyd said reassuringly.

Chapter 17

Hampshire

Lydia paced her study again, pushing her glasses up her nose, a habit she had when she was agitated. "I hope we have done the right thing."

"It is a little too late to be considering this now," Matthew, the Earl of Fleetwood and her husband, said. "She should be arriving soon."

"That is not a helpful comment to make," Lydia huffed at him.

"Come here," Matthew said, pulling her down onto his knee. "We talked about this. It is the best route to take, the only way to solve everyone's problems, for we could not continue going on as we have been."

Lydia rested her head on his shoulder. "I know. I am just afraid that Alice will hate me when she realises why I have sent for her."

"She will probably thank you, but perhaps not immediately," Matthew said with a laugh when Lydia punched him in the arm.

"You are determined to make me feel worse about this, are you not?"

"Not at all. I am just pointing out the obvious, we both know who he needs in order to reach him. We have tried everything else we could think of to no avail."

"I know you are right. I just hope that I am not adding to Alice's hurt by dragging her here under false pretences. Knowing she will be worried does not sit well with me, but I am convinced she would not have come if she knew the real reason we need her."

"She seems to have strength of character. She must have to be the one to turn Avril's head, for he would not be attracted to anyone insipid. He needed someone who was not afraid to stand up to him, and from what you said, she certainly isn't."

Only moving from her husband's embrace when a knock disturbed them, she stood and nodded at the footman who announced Alice's arrival. "I am so happy to see you!" Lydia exclaimed, wrapping Alice in an embrace and hoping that her friend had not heard the snort of amusement at her words from her husband. "I hope your journey was untroubled?"

"Yes, very uneventful," Alice said, pulling away from Lydia and looking closely at her. "What is it? What has happened that you need my help?"

"I am so glad you came, but let us have some tea before we start to discuss the details," Lydia said quickly.

Stepping back, Alice looked at Matthew. "Why is she delaying matters and not telling me what is amiss?"

Matthew smiled at Alice. "You know I am not foolish enough to cross her, so I am afraid I cannot help you in this instance, but it is nice to see you looking well."

She glared at Matthew in mock annoyance. "That is reassuring, as I was recovering from a head wound the last time we met." Alice turned her attention back to Lydia. "I would imagine my portmanteau is still in the hallway. I can quite easily call for the carriage and leave."

"I think being famous has gone to her head. She was never so difficult previously," Lydia huffed at her husband, but admitted defeat at Alice's expression. "Fine. I give in, you had better sit down, and this is not a delaying tactic."

Alice did as she was bid, a sudden sense of dread filling her stomach. She had been relieved to see Lydia and Matthew looking so well, and although it had not been mentioned, it was clear that nothing had gone wrong with Matthew's sister, or he would not be funning with them. Wondering what could possibly be amiss, Alice braced herself for bad news.

Lydia took a breath. "Captain Avril is here."

"What?" Alice almost shouted.

"He has been here some days, and we did not know what else to do other than send for you," Lydia said.

"Send for his wife," Alice said bitterly.

"If we knew who she was or where they were living, we might have been able to do that, but he is drunk most of the time and mumbles nonsense. He is much changed since the last time we saw him," Lydia said.

"Why is nothing simple with that man?" Alice huffed. "I do not know where he is living, but I can give you his parents' address. You could have asked me that in a letter."

"We decided to contact you because on the few times we can get close enough, his drunken ramblings are about you," Matthew said. "We were hoping you might be the one to be able to stop his acts of self-destruction."

Alice rubbed her hands over her face. "I must really have done something evil that I cannot remember, for I swear I am being tortured."

"I am sorry, but we could not send him on his way without trying to help. He is still technically eligible for our support," Lydia said gently. Her work with the soldiers who had not been able to return home after their service was no longer needed to protect the country against the threat of invasion had meant she had seen all sorts of problems the men were facing. "He is hurting, Alice, and I think it is to do with you."

Springing from her seat, Alice moved behind the chair, clinging onto the back as if for support. "He chose to be honourable and marry the woman who had betrayed him. If there are any residual feelings for me, I am sure he will get over them. He made his choice, Lydia, and I was not it."

Matthew looked at Alice with sympathy. "I am sorry we have had to bring you into this. It must be extremely hard for you."

"You cannot imagine," Alice responded.

"I think I have a little knowledge of what you are feeling," Matthew said, aiming a smile at Lydia. "Ours was not the easy journey I would have hoped, and I still have no recollection about a lot of my past."

"I apologise. I was being selfish and unfeeling; you have gone through far worse than I have."

"It is understandable to be hurt, but for your sake as well as his, I think you should see him and then decide whether to leave him to wallow or to help him," Matthew reasoned.

"Half of me wants to run to him and fling myself into his arms; the other half wants to run away and never stop," Alice said honestly. "I will see him. I cannot in all conscience just ignore him if he is truly hurting, whatever the cause of it. He did make his decision, though, and I am not sure what I can do to help."

"At least if you try, we will know that we have done everything we can," Lydia said. "Thank you for at least attempting to bring him out of his stupor. We really were at a loss at what to do to help him."

"Where is he?"

"He has insisted that he stays in the stable, declaring he is not fit for anything else," Lydia said.

"The foolish man!" Alice said, exasperated. "I will do what I can."

"I am sure he will be thankful," Lydia said gently.

"I am doing this for you, not him," Alice said. "He should not be causing so much inconvenience for everyone. I might as well go straight there. The sooner I get this over, the faster I can return to London."

As Alice walked out of the study, her step forceful, Lydia looked at Matthew with a shocked expression. "I was teasing when I said that she used to be very obliging, but this is not a side of Alice that I have seen before. She has never been so – dismissive of someone who is troubled."

"He hurt her by choosing another. I cannot imagine either of us feeling benevolent to the other if we had married someone else."

"No." Lydia shuddered. "When I was told you were going to make a match for the sake of your family's promises already made, I was beside myself thinking that I had lost you."

"Yes, and you gave me short shrift when I visited," Matthew said with raised eyebrows. "I had spoken of how wonderful you were to Emily, and when we arrived, you were little more than a harridan."

"Brute! I have since apologised to you both on numerous occasions. It was not my finest hour," Lydia said, hands on hips.

Matthew stood and pulled her to him. "I might have been confused, but I never stopped loving you, even then."

"Neither had I," Lydia said. "It really was the worst time of my life."

"Let us hope that Alice and Avril have the same happy conclusion as we have."

"If Captain Avril has married another, there cannot be."

"True. I feel for Alice, I really do, but I cannot help hoping she can help him in some way."

"So do I."

***

Alice was thankful that James did not notice her immediately as she stood in the opening of the final stall in the stable block. Lydia and Matthew had warned her that he had changed, but she had not expected him to look as he did now.

When she had first met him, he was getting a bath, as the housekeeper in Hesketh Hall insisted with all the soldiers who came to stay. It was unusual that Alice be there, but after a tussle with him not releasing his kilt to the housekeeper, Lydia had been sought out for her help, and Alice had followed. It was the moment when Alice's world had been rocked by the sight before her, he was a large beast of a man, but there was also mischief in him and a sense of outrageous fun. She had never met a man who had turned her head so much or so quickly, and getting to know him over the following weeks had only increased her feelings.

Now, though, he was slumped in a corner, empty gin jug by his side; he was filthy, had lost a lot of weight and wore an unruly beard. He looked as if he was dozing, and Alice took a moment to steady herself. Seeing him had brought everything back, but in addition to the feelings she had been trying to repress, she now had the overwhelming urge to rush to him and try to fix whatever was ailing him.

Knowing that he would not respond well to anything other than being forceful with him, she set her shoulders. “That kilt looks in worse condition than it ever has. Your grandfather is probably rolling in his grave,” she said, folded arms, leaning on the wooden structure which separated each stall.

James blinked a few times and squinted at Alice. “What are you doing ’ere, lassie?” His words were slurred, and his head seemed unable to remain upright.

“More importantly, what the devil are you doing here?” Alice demanded, blushing at the use of her language but knowing she had to shock him into action.

“I didnae know where else to go,” James responded candidly.

“And you decided to stay foxed day and night and sleep in a stable. That is not one of your best plans.”

“I just wanted to disappear, but every time I think or do anything, it reminds me of you. Blasted pixie, cannae stop thinking about ye, even when I am foxed.”

Alice heard a sound behind her to see Matthew and Lydia hovering. She rolled her eyes at them and turned back to James. “You have two hours to clean yourself up, get rid of that beard and make yourself presentable enough to have tea with me in the library.”

“I cannae do that.”

"I will see you in two hours. Do not be late, or I will seek you out, and it will not be pleasant. And for goodness sake, get that kilt washed!"

Alice walked past Lydia and Matthew. "I hope Mrs Hill will not have the same issues she had last time he was here. If she does, just send for me. I will be waiting in the library, trying to work out what I am going to say to him to make him see that he cannot continue in this way."

"Thank you," Lydia said. "You have already got more sentences out of him than anyone else. Even the other soldiers have not been able to get through his mumblings."

"Let us hope my influence continues, or you could have him as a strange guest until he drinks himself to death," Alice said.

***

Ten minutes before the two hours was up, James walked into the library, dressed neatly and clean-shaven. Alice took a moment to appreciate him. He had relinquished the kilt, and as it was the first time she had ever seen him in anything other than the kilt, she noted that he looked every inch the gentleman in his dark breeches, flowered waistcoat and dark frockcoat. The blue in his eyes and his blonde hair seemed to be accentuated by the dark clothing he wore. Knowing that Mrs Hill kept a large supply of clothes to be given to the soldiers when they first arrived, she was only surprised that there was clothing in the stocks big enough to fit him.

Sitting opposite Alice, glower firmly in place, he kept his eyes lowered. "Are ye happy now?"

"Not in the slightest, but that is a moot point at the moment," Alice responded. "Tea?"

"I would rather have some whiskey."

"I am sure you would. Unfortunately, I do not wish to converse with a drunken wastrel," Alice said primly, pouring the tea. "I will add lots of sugar; perhaps that will sweeten your mood." She ignored the growl he gave and handed him a cup.

"There is no point to whatever it is you are trying to do," James said, emptying the cup in one gulp.

Alice had to refrain from laughing at the sight of James holding the tiny teacup, but she dutifully filled his cup once more and handed it back to him, which caused another glower to be aimed at her. When he had taken the cup, Alice sat back, her hands on her lap, and she looked at him fully. Her usual smile was nowhere to be seen, her frown a match for his.

"I have been brought here to try and help you, but I am not sure I want to," she said.

Looking in surprise at her, he put his cup into the saucer with a clatter. "Well, leave me be then."

"I cannot do that when your actions are interfering with the vital work of my friends."

"I can leave," James said, starting to rise.

"Sit!" Alice commanded, and to her utter surprise, he complied. "I do not care if it is my business or not, your actions have caused me to be involved, and I will do what I can to help."

"Leave me be, Alice."

He had rarely called her by her given name, and she realised how much he was hurting. She changed her tone and spoke to him as she always had. "What has happened? I thought you would be settled with your family by now." She tried not to sound bitter but was not sure she succeeded.

A hollow laugh was all the sound he made at first, putting his head in his hands and sitting forward. Alice waited until he sat up, looking haunted.

"It was all a ploy, lassie. She had cheated on me before I even left for the war. Nothing happened that last night as she claimed; he was Simon's son."

"Oh lord!"

"I think she was created by the devil. She had everything planned out, how Hamish was going to come to an untimely end and then the boy would inherit," James said, his tone dead.

"What a thing to have considered!" Alice exclaimed.

"The fact that he was to inherit from an uncle who doted on him was irrelevant; the title was clearly what she wanted. Thank goodness Drew had overheard her speaking to Simon and him admitting the child was his."

Alice was stunned, her mind racing at what James had explained. She did not have words to offer. What could she say? That she was sorry he was not married to Constance? She could not be so hypocritical, but there was one thing she did wonder about, yet she could not utter the words quite yet.

Eventually, James broke the silence. "I cannae believe that I ever trusted anything that woman uttered. She was a conniving liar and nothing more."

"You will get no disagreement from me over that," Alice said, which brought a smile to his face for the first time since she had seen him. "It does not explain why you returned to Hesketh Hall." *And not me*, but she managed to refrain from speaking the words.

"I wanted to get away," he said. "It didnae feel right staying there. I just wanted to be as far away from her as I could be."

"Oh, I see."

James jumped from his seat and stormed across the room. Alice thought he was going to leave her without saying anything else, but he turned as he reached the door. "I wanted you, I will always want you, lassie, but you made it quite clear that you would not accept second best, and I respect that about you. There are no second measures, and you deserve nothing less. You need someone who will always put you first, I did not do that in the most spectacular way, and I will never forgive myself for it."

"Yet it was me who persuaded you not to get a special licence," Alice pointed out.

"Aye, and how would that have turned out? Me having to jilt you? I despise myself enough at the moment. I can only be thankful that we did not go further. Go and live your life, lassie. You are better off without me, I have already proved that."

Alice was left alone in the library as he marched out of the house. She had no idea where he was going and made no attempt to follow him. Moving away from the tea tray, she picked up a book, blindly looking at it until Lydia disturbed her.

"You worked your magic on Captain Avril," she said as she entered the room.

"Did I? I have no idea how."

"He has just barged into the study and told Matthew that he needs work and the harder the better. He must have decided that you were worth fighting for and is straightening himself out."

Alice laughed. "If you brought me out here hoping that would be the conclusion from him seeing me again, then you are to be disappointed. He will not be courting me, now or in the future, and I admit to being foolish enough to hope that he might. Not only am I stupid enough to fall for him a first time, I am willing to put myself through it once more when I find out he is not married at all and everything he was told were lies."

"Really? You can tell me more about why he did not marry later. I do not understand why he would not come straight to you."

"I told him in the past that I would not accept second best. It was actually in this house," Alice said, remembering how saying the words had nearly broken her heart after just experiencing the most wonderful kisses she had ever had. "He says he respects me for it and would not expect me to go back on my principles for him."

"And you did not argue against him?"

"What is the point? Have him think I am akin to Constance in saying one thing and meaning another? No, I have lost him, and the only good thing to come out of this visit is that at least I know for sure now."

"Oh, Alice. I am so sorry you feel this way. Give him some time; he will change his mind when he is around you more."

"I cannot remain here. I need to go back home."

"No! Please stay," Lydia pleaded.

"I will return soon, perhaps when he has left," Alice said. "I need to go back to London. The ironic thing is there is a man in London who dotes on me, wants me on whatever terms I lay down, even if I never love him and yet he would spend every day trying to make me happy."

"Who is it?"

"My publisher," Alice said with a glimmer of a smile. "There would be no pressure for me to give up my writing. It really is a perfect match."

"But—?"

"I feel absolutely nothing for him and never will. Even though there is no hope with James, for I do know how belligerent he is that he will remain steadfast in thinking that I would never accept him, I could not marry another."

"I wish I knew what to do to make this better," Lydia said, embracing Alice.

"There is nothing any of us can do. It is time I left."

"Please stay until tomorrow," Lydia begged. "We can at least enjoy each other's company."

"If you promise not to try any matchmaking, I will stay until the morning." Alice was drained and wanted to sleep, though she thought she would not. It would be easier and safer staying at Hesketh Hall than setting out so late in the day.

"I promise you will not see him unless you want to."

"My heart does; my head does not."

"At least you are being honest," Lydia said. "Come, Matthew will want to know all about your foray into the publishing world."

Alice smiled. "It is not as exciting as you might imagine."

"Being the pet of the patronesses is not exciting! You have either become very difficult to please or you are funning with me," Lydia scoffed.

"Fine! Rather than exciting, I would say it is more terrifying than anything else."

"Now that I can believe."

Chapter 18

James had never worked harder in his life. Matthew had sent him to a farm on the outskirts of the village which had a new tenant but had been neglected for a long time. He revelled in the work, though it meant his body collapsed exhausted into the chamber which he shared with two others, now that he had accepted he should no longer remain in the stables. The problem was that no matter how hard he worked, how much he tried to forget her, all he could think of was Alice.

What kind of idiot was he that she had come back into his life and he had walked away from her? He should have begged her to take him on whatever terms she would accept, instead he had been an utter fool and deserved the misery he felt, every moment of every day and for most of the night.

He saw Matthew and Lydia regularly, they very often invited him to dine with them, but there was always an undercurrent of awkwardness in the room. None of them able to speak about Alice, although both Lydia and James wished to.

Returning to Hesketh Hall one evening, sweat-soaked and exhausted, James was waved at by a group of the soldiers. Crossing to them, he nodded in acknowledgement. They were chattering excitedly, and James stood listening for a moment.

"Where did you hear this?" he asked.

"Will here was told by Mr Henshaw, the farmer he works for, the East India Company are actively looking for experienced military men to go to India. There are problems over there with the locals, which the company is determined to get rid of, but they need men on the ground," Jack said, his face lit up with excitement.

"Do they now? And are you going?" James asked.

"Definitely. It will mean we are back on full pay and doing something useful," Jack said.

"Helping the people in this area is of use," James said.

"It is, but we are treated like children. We can't have our money until we leave, apart from a small amount, we are watched and reported on; it isn't right," Jack groused.

James smiled. "I know some who have been here, where close watching was the only thing which kept the valuables in the house." He received scowls for his words but was not intimidated by the men he towered over.

"Typical officer," Will muttered darkly.

James slapped him on his back. "Who would give you more rules than you would ever get here. Do not look a gift horse in the mouth. This was a haven when you needed it. I will not have this place or Lady Fleetwood bad-mouthed."

"She is a saint. Meant no disrespect," William said, trying to disguise the pain he was in from the slap James had given him.

"Glad to hear it." James walked away from the men. He was not one for making friendships with the others in the house, he was not unfriendly, just distant. He entered the house, frown firmly in place.

Matthew walked down the stairs. "Avril, what is amiss?"

"I've just been told that the East India Company are recruiting for India," James said.

"Yes, it was reported yesterday in the paper. News travels fast. Are we to have an empty house soon?"

"I think you will lose some, and then if they survive, they will be back more damaged than they are now," James said.

"I take from that you will not be joining them?" Matthew said with a grin.

"It is something to think about certainly," James said, his frown returning. "There is little keeping me here."

"I never had you down as someone who would give up without a fight," Matthew said in surprise that James would consider leaving the country and the chance of seeing Alice in the future.

Scowling at him, James huffed. "I feel battered. I do not want anything else to add to it."

"So instead of facing and solving what is troubling you, you are effectively running away," Matthew said.

"I did not think on seeing you that I was going to receive a lecture," James said roughly.

Matthew held his hands up. "No lecture, censure or anything from me, just stating what I see."

"Pfft," James said, heading up the stairs and passing Matthew with a silent glower.

Matthew smiled as he walked the remainder of the stairs, but he sought out Lydia to tell her about what some of the men were considering. They would be able to accept new men into the house if some left. It was such a popular scheme that there was an unofficial waiting list, with most still living rough until there was space for them.

***

Coming into the house a few days after the news had broken about the recruitment by the company, James was stopped from joining the men in the large dining room. He had avoided dining with Matthew and Lydia, not because he was sulking, but talking about Alice, even indirectly, made him ache more than he already was.

Lydia stepped out of the smaller breakfast room that she and Matthew used as their dining room, separate from the men. It worked well as it gave both some privacy.

"Ah, Captain Avril, please join us. We have a visitor who is most keen to see you."

James was frustrated when his heart gave a lurch of hope at her words. He frowned, his inner turmoil spilling onto his face. He did not deserve her, she wanted someone better than he could ever hope to be, but his blasted body and mind had reacted at the sliver of hope that she had returned to Hesketh Hall for him.

Following Lydia into the cosy but comfortable breakfast room, he was surprised and shamefully, a little disappointed when he saw Hamish seated at the table.

"What is wrong?" he demanded of his brother, sure there could only be bad news to report if his brother had tracked him down.

"And hello to you too," Hamish said sardonically. "You have lost weight and look haggard since you left us. I see this working lifestyle clearly does not agree with you."

"Fortunately for me, it does not matter. I am no dandy." James scowled back at his brother.

"Neither am I, dear brother. I would consider myself a Corinthian at least."

Lydia watched the brothers interact with a smile on her face. She had no siblings, so was amused to watch the toing and froing.

"Please take a seat, Captain Avril. I am sure you have a lot to chat about. I will leave you in peace."

"There is no need to go on my account," Hamish said. "From the looks of things, you will be by far the more appealing conversationalist than my brother. I do often wonder if my mother had a dalliance. As you can see, there is very little that would cause people to consider us brothers."

Laughing and shaking her head at Hamish, Lydia spoke. “Oh, I can already see the similarities.”

“You wound me, my lady,” Hamish said, hand on his heart.

“Now you have turned into Drew,” James muttered.

“Which would horrify our brother. I must remember to tell him when I return home.”

“On that note, I will leave you be,” Lydia said. “I am sorry that we cannot offer you accommodation, sir, but there is an inn not too far away that is respectable.”

“Do not concern yourself over my comfort. I arrived in the area yesterday and set up quite comfortably in the inn,” Hamish said.

“Bringing your own sheets, valet and a carriage full of clothes, no doubt,” James mocked.

“Of course. Most would consider us Scots to be little more than savages, and with you walking around in such a state, I can understand why. It is my duty to show them we are not all unrefined beasts.”

“Please stay and join us for supper tonight,” Lydia said. “My husband will appreciate your company, and of course you must join us too, Captain Avril.”

“To be the sacrificial lamb for my brother’s barbs?” James asked.

“You could never be considered a helpless lamb, Captain.” Lydia smiled before leaving the brothers alone.

“How did you find me here?” James demanded. “What has really brought you from home?”

"Questions, questions, be seated and we can share this exquisite brandy our fine hostess has supplied." Hamish poured James a glass, the action making James reluctantly take a seat.

"Be straight talking for once in your life," James said, taking a drink of the brandy, appreciating the warmth as it travelled through his body.

"You can be such a bore sometimes," Hamish complained but sat forward in his seat. "Our darling brother has never stopped talking about being published since he met Miss Boyd, so I went to London to try and speak to the publisher Miss Boyd has achieved success with."

"I am surprised you could be bothered to stir yourself to act on Drew's behalf," James said.

"It is tiresome to have younger brothers, but I am expecting Mary to be worse when it is her turn to be ravaged with angst over something or other," Hamish said. "If I get the troubled soul of our family... Oh wait, we are cursed to have two in our family, I forget about your melancholy. Anyway, if I solved one of Drew's problems, perhaps he would stop whining quite so much. I do like a peaceful house."

James cracked out a laugh. "This from the man who introduced me to bawdy houses. You do not like quiet; you were as bad as any of the other foxed visitors."

"There is a time and a place, brother. I also had some business I wanted to follow up with and, unfortunately, I could not get it resolved, so I thought I would come and visit you before heading out to the continent for a brief sojourn." Hamish looked almost wary at uttering the words and stiffened as if waiting for James to confess something or make a comment.

"You have already been on your Grand Tour. Why do you want to go again? I thought it was time you were settling down and producing an heir."

"As it seems you and Drew are unable to produce your own offspring and leave me to enjoy my life of dissipation, I have come to the conclusion that I must marry." James had not picked up on Hamish's discomfort, and he was able to relax a little and revert to form.

"And you cannot find a wife the length and breadth of this country? That is so typical of you."

"Not at all," Hamish said, his face trying to disguise an emotion James could not work out but mistakenly presumed that nothing serious was amiss. "I just wish to explore all the opportunities, that is all. It has to be the right person to take over as Lady Kirkbride when the time comes."

"For once, I agree with you, brought home even more so when I realised Constance had designs on the title. It would have been a crime to have her residing over the estate," James ground out.

"At least I would not have been there to see it, as she was determined to get me out of the way," Hamish said, quite unperturbed at the thought that Constance's plans to marry James needed Hamish dead before she could inherit the title.

"I am not convinced that my life would have been safe for long. I think the boy would have been easier to bully than I was."

"She got a shock when you returned and were no longer the compliant puppy you had been before you left."

"Puppy?" James spluttered out.

"Maybe a Great Dane of a puppy, but still one nonetheless." Hamish laughed at his brother's incredulous expression. "It is nothing to be ashamed of. Falling in love is supposed to be the most wonderful feeling in the world."

"And the most painful," James said, immediately feeling the ache which was always in the background since Alice was no longer in his life.

"Are you going to remain here indefinitely? It is safe to return home; the dreaded Constance has moved in with Cameron's uncle. I feel sorry for the boy and the man, but rather she be there than in our locality."

"Aye, she is better off with them," James said. "I did not know what I was going to do or where I was going to go, but I have been told of an interesting option."

"Tell me more."

"You have still not told me about what happened in London with the publisher," James pointed out.

"That is not as interesting as hearing what mad scheme you are intent on," Hamish said, dismissing his youngest brother's work.

"It is no mad scheme," James said. "The East India Company want men to go over and help keep order in India. It makes sense for me to offer my services; there is nothing to keep me here."

"Is there not? That is interesting."

"Do not be clever with me. I have not the patience for it," James snapped.

"Fine. Why are you going to another conflict when there is absolutely no need to put yourself through it? I can understand why you went to the Peninsular, even to the Americas, and then France, but this? Are you determined to push fate so much that you will eventually run out of luck?" Hamish asked, no longer funning with his brother.

"I didnae know you cared," James could not help teasing. "It will pay well and it gives me a purpose."

"That is some consolation when you are dead on a foreign battlefield, if not killed by yellow fever first. James, I know you are unhappy, but this is not the way to solve it."

"I am going to London in two days," James shrugged. "I am going straight to the East India Offices."

"I could shake you sometimes."

"I would like to see ye try," James laughed.

"You might be the size of a bear, but you have the brain of a peasant. I despair of you, I really do."

"I have made my decision."

"And yet again, it is the wrong one," Hamish said, pushing his chair back from the table and standing up. “Excuse me, I need to go for a walk or I will try and punch you, whether I end up on my rear or not. You absolute fool.”

James was left staring at an open door, surprised at his brother’s outburst but feeling that Hamish had assessed him correctly.

Chapter 19

London – a week earlier.

Alice had sent a note to Mr Mortimer as soon as she had returned home, excusing herself from not having had the chance to think about his proposal and asking for more time. Worried that she was leading him on by asking for longer to consider did not rest easy with her, but she could not face another emotional encounter just yet.

Inviting Serena and Frances for lunch, she explained what had happened at Hesketh Hall. "He was so changed and, in a way, different from the man he had been."

"He has had a lot of turmoil recently, it is not too much of a surprise that he is affected by it. I saw how he was with you, and that is a man smitten," Serena said.

"Not enough to look beyond the foolish words I uttered when I thought life was far less complicated," Alice said. "How I wish I could take them back now, but the silly man has latched onto them, and so that is it."

"Did you not try to convince him that you no longer thought that way?" Frances asked.

"No. To be honest, I did not know what to do," Alice finally admitted aloud. "The irony of my lack of ability to think of something to say that would change his mindset is not lost on me. How can I, who writes conversations every day, be lost for words?" The last came out more anguished than she had intended, her eyes filling with tears at her frustration with herself.

"Oh Alice, he will rally and see sense," Serena said. "He had a troubled time at home; just give him a little while longer."

"How long do I live in hope for? He is all I can think of, and I know I cannot go on like this. I annoy myself when I am constantly mooning over him."

"Have you decided about Mr Mortimer?" Serena asked.

"There has never been anything to decide, not compared to James," Alice said. "I thought I should listen to Archie, who said that Mr Mortimer offered me the perfect package, and for anyone being sensible about their future it would be."

"Why would you settle for a proposal when you do not need to?" Serena asked. "You are an independent woman who will become more financially secure than you were before. Why enter a marriage you do not wish to have?"

Alice shrugged. "Archie pointed out that the future could be a lonely place for a spinster."

"But you are not a spinster, you are a Bluestocking who is more than capable of taking control of her life and is surrounded by friends. I do not understand this need to marry. What with Julia, Lydia, and now you, there will be no Bluestockings left," Serena said.

Frances laughed at her friend. "They are still Bluestockings, just married ones."

"It just seems that we were all happy, and all of a sudden, marriages are thrown into the mix and everyone is upset. Julia and Lydia had bumpy rides to get their husbands, and now yours is not a straightforward path. It all seems too hard to me. I am happy the way I am," Serena said.

"Until you meet the right man," Frances argued back. "I cannot say that I am looking for a husband, but I am not against it either."

Serena grumbled but was interrupted by a footman.

"Miss Boyd, there is a Mr Avril to see you," the footman said.

Alice lurched to her feet. "Mr Avril? Here? Show him in!"

Serena and Frances stood. "We will leave you be."

"What do I say?" Alice asked in an urgent whisper before turning towards the door to greet the unexpected guest. "Oh," she said, deflated.

"That is not the usual greeting I would hope to achieve when entering a room full of beautiful women," Hamish said.

"Frances, this is the honourable Mr Avril, elder brother of Captain Avril. Mr Avril, please let me introduce my two friends, Miss Formby you already know, and Miss Somers is another of our Bluestocking Club."

"Ladies." Hamish bowed. "It is a pleasure to see you again, Miss Formby, and Miss Somers, delighted to make your acquaintance."

"Please, Mr Avril, take a seat. You find us gossiping over our lunch, which you are more than welcome to join."

"Thank you, coffee will be perfectly sufficient," Hamish said, taking a seat. "Are you well, Miss Boyd?"

"I am. I hope your family are in good health?" Alice asked.

"Yes, although I had hoped you had some news about one of them," Hamish said, accepting the coffee supplied by the footman.

"Oh?" Alice asked, refusing to submit to the twinkle of amusement in Hamish's eyes.

"My brother left home soon after you departed, and we do not know where he is. I was hoping he had sought you out, but at your reaction to my entrance, I am now presuming not," Hamish said.

"I have not seen your brother in London, but I do know that he is or was residing at Hesketh Hall," Alice said.

"Why on earth has he gone there when you are here?" Hamish blurted out before seeming to recall himself. "I beg pardon, Miss Boyd. It seems I am surrounded by foolish family members."

"How is Drew?" Alice smiled.

Hamish laughed. "Hoping that your connection with your publisher will give him the advantage when I go to beg the man to publish his ramblings."

"Oh, I doubt my opinion or recommendation would sway Mr Mortimer," Alice said.

"Surely he has not cast you off? My sister has done nothing but rave about your writing since Miss Formby kindly sent her a set of volumes."

Alice smiled. "No, he has not, not yet at least. Is that why you have travelled to London?"

"That and to seek out the elusive James," Hamish said. "It appears I will be trailing to Hesketh Hall in order to see him."

"I am afraid so."

"I will be happy to introduce you to Mr Mortimer," Serena said, taking pity on Alice, which caused a look of gratitude from her friend. "I have met him, and he knows of the connection between Alice and I."

"That would be very kind of you, thank you. As repayment, would the three of you, and anyone else you would care to invite, wish to join me for the evening at Vauxhall Gardens?" Hamish asked. "I admit to liking their firework displays whenever I am in the area."

"We were thinking of going there ourselves and asking Serena's cousin to accompany us," Frances said. "It would be lovely to have you join us."

"Ben? I would enjoy reacquainting myself with him. Then it is settled. I shall collect you from here at eight tonight if that is acceptable?"

"Perfect," Frances said with a smile.

"Excellent. Until tonight, ladies." Hamish emptied his cup, bowed and left the ladies alone.

"Well! If Captain Avril is half as handsome as his brother, I can see why you have lost your heart to him!" Frances said.

"His brother is far more appealing than Mr Avril," Alice said airily but smiled when Frances and Serena laughed at her comment. "Only Serena can be the unbiased judge."

"Oh no you do not," Serena said, shaking her head. "I am not saying a word on either brother for danger of being unable to say the right thing, whatever I say."

"That means she prefers Mr Avril," Frances teased. "Just think, you could marry both brothers and end as sisters!"

"I think you are forgetting one thing," Serena interjected. "Neither brother is here declaring his undying affection. Sorry for being so brutal, Alice."

"As you are speaking the truth, I cannot be critical of your words," Alice said with a shrug.

"At least we have a lovely evening to look forward to," Frances said. "Now all we have to do is plan what we are to wear."

***

Alice liked Hamish in his own right, but she also wanted to speak to him about James. Though she had seen him more recently than his brother, she hoped Hamish would be able to help her understand some of his brother's decisions.

Travelling in the Kirkbride carriage, Hamish regaled them with tales of his exploits which kept them shocked and amused throughout the journey to the famous entertainment venue. Hamish had secured a box for them all in a prime position.

"I have ordered food and drink to be brought here soon," Hamish said. "I do not wish for your parents to be chasing after me for not looking after you all well."

"I think that having two footmen and both of you protecting us will suffice," Serena said of Hamish and Ben, who had happily come on the trip once he heard Hamish was in town. "We are hardly just out of the schoolroom."

"But there are rogues and vagabonds who will try their best to lead astray pretty young women."

"Some of us might want to be led astray," Frances said, causing Hamish to laugh.

"I like your friends, Miss Boyd."

"I am quite fond of them myself," Alice responded.

When the food arrived, Hamish took the opportunity to speak to Alice while the other three were choosing what delicacies they wanted from the vast array provided.

"How was my brother when you saw him last?" he asked, all seriousness.

"Thinner and looking more troubled than usual," Alice said.

"Things must be bad," Hamish muttered to himself. "Do you know what happened after you left?"

"I know that the child is not his, and there has been no marriage," Alice said without emotion.

"No, thankfully he found out the truth before it was too late. It was a relief to all his family that he was not forced to marry Constance. To be honest, Miss Boyd, I thought he had left to find you once he was free from her grasp."

"Apparently not."

"But you have seen him?"

"Yes, my friend contacted me for help. He was wallowing in jugs of gin and living in a stable."

"Good God! I despair of my family sometimes, I truly do," Hamish said, looking frustrated. "I need to box his ears as I did before he turned into a walking giant."

Alice laughed. "Yes, I can imagine his return attack would hurt. I think that I left him in a better frame of mind, although I do not really know. He certainly looked more presentable, at least, as I refused to converse with him whilst he stunk and had an out-of-control beard. It did him no favours to appear so wild."

Hamish smiled, despite Alice's words revealing that his brother was in a poor frame of mind. "Miss Boyd, I now understand why you have attracted the name pixie from my brother. I think underneath all his bluster, he is a little bit afraid of you."

Bursting out a very unladylike guffaw, Alice looked around the box with some embarrassment, which increased at the curious looks which were aimed in their direction. "I wish I was scary, for I could demand he tell me why he did not come to me when he found out Constance was being false for her own gain."

"He is a complicated man, I am not about to offer excuses, but I think when he returned from Waterloo, he was relying on his future with that blasted woman to remove some of the damage being at war for so long had caused. It was more than a double blow when he lost both Constance and Simon. I can only presume that he no longer trusts his own judgement."

"Hamish, come and tell Serena that a walk in the gardens is not a good idea for an innocent miss," Ben said from across the box.

"For goodness sake! I am nearly seven and twenty!" Serena snapped at her cousin.

"In that case, allow me the honour of escorting you along the pathways," Hamish said, offering his arm to Serena. "Let us see if we can shock a woman of the world by the goings-on we might come across."

Alice noticed the scowl that Serena aimed in Hamish's direction and suppressed a smile. Hamish might be handsome and smooth-talking, but it seemed that Serena was not impressed.

"I would like to go for a stroll. I do feel a little on show when in one of these boxes," Frances said once she had finished her food.

"We are here to see and be seen," Ben pointed out.

"I would rather be the one seeing," Frances said. She was the quietest and most reserved of the Bluestockings, happiest when in her garden.

"In that case, let me escort you both, and we shall be the ones perusing who is here and with whom," Ben said gallantly.

Frances grinned. "Now that sounds like fun."

The three strolled along the pathways, lights discreetly giving some illumination to the walkers, though there was enough darkness for assignations to take place. Both Frances and Alice had cause to giggle when they walked by a particularly noisy area.

"I knew this was a mistake," Ben groaned as both of them choked on a laugh.

"It is very enlightening," Alice said, trying to sound serious and failing.

"This is going to appear in your next book," Ben said with resignation.

"The number of people who presume people or things are interesting enough to appear in a book can very often be completely misguided, but in this case, I think you can guarantee that Vauxhall Pleasure Gardens will be mentioned at some point."

"I blame Serena for this. You were happy in the box until she became restless."

At Ben's words, there was a squeak of alarm, and when the threesome stepped past a nearby bush, they all came to a shocked stop. Before them were Hamish and Serena, and it was clear from both of their demeanours that they had just been interrupted kissing each other.

"What the devil!" Ben snapped, pulling away from Frances and Alice and marching over to Hamish and Serena. "What in damnation is going on?"

"Nothing, and mind your language," Serena hissed at her cousin. Even in the darkness, it was clear she was blushing.

"I will not mind my language when this cur has just compromised my cousin! Is this how you repay friendship? I will meet you for this!"

Hamish looked about to step forward, but Serena moved between them. "You will do nothing so ridiculous, and you can lower your voice. The last thing we need is for someone to hear you shouting compromise all over the place, and then there really will be trouble. For you," she said to Ben.

He spluttered in disbelief, grabbing Serena's arm to pull her away, but Hamish stopped him. "Unhand her. I am not going to stand by while you hurt her, no matter that we were in the wrong. Let us return to the box and calm down."

Ben landed the first blow unexpectedly on Hamish's jaw, snapping his head back, but Hamish was ready for the second punch and blocked it. "Damn you, man! Stop this before your cousin is truly ruined."

"You absolute cur, I will destroy you for this!" Ben snarled, moving to continue the fight.

"Then you will have ruined your cousin in the process. Is that what you want?" Hamish growled in return.

"Will you please stop!" Serena hissed at them both. "There is no need for this."

"There is every need when you could have been seen by anyone," Ben countered.

"Then it is fortunate that we were not," Serena huffed. "Ben, stop. I have not been compromised. I am not going to marry Mr Avril, so you can breathe easy." She did not notice the look Hamish shot in her direction, but his posture stiffened enough that Alice and Frances exchanged a look.

"Who has not been compromised?" A voice behind them jolted them all from the intensity of their exchange.

"L-Lady Jersey, how nice it is to see you," Alice stuttered.

"I expect not if there is scandal brewing amongst you. When are we to expect a wedding? And I hope it is not yours, Miss Boyd. I would hate to think that our attentions have been wasted."

"No, I am not marrying," Alice said, her insides panicking as she tried to think of a way to distract the woman who looked more like a bird watching its prey.

"Glad to hear it. So, which one of your friends is the one risking her reputation?" Lady Jersey looked at Frances and Serena. "It must be you," she said, pointing at Serena but not giving any clue why she came to her conclusion. "It appears I interrupted a fight. Do not stop on my account, gentlemen. I have seen the best of them fight. A mill is always diverting."

"There is no fight, my lady," Serena said stiffly. "And there is to be no wedding."

Lady Jersey had been looking slightly amused until Serena's words, but at them, any hint of a smile disappeared. "No wedding, but it would appear that you have been compromised, I and others heard the words."

Serena flushed even deeper red. "It was a misunderstanding, that is all."

"A woman ruined is never a misunderstanding. You are uttering some very dangerous words, young lady. I suggest you think carefully before you suffer the consequences."

Serena stood to her full height, which was only average for a woman, but she lifted her chin, clearly standing her ground. "I am not going to marry someone just because of one kiss. If that is unacceptable, then I am sorry, but show me a woman who has not been kissed before she was wed and probably not to the man she eventually marries."

"Serena!" Ben groaned, his hand over his face as if he could no longer watch what was happening.

"I see. In that case, goodbye, Miss Boyd. I suggest you consider the company you keep before we next meet." Lady Jersey looked Serena up and down, and turning her back on her, she walked away.

"She has just given you the cut direct," Frances said in a faint voice.

"I know." Serena's eyes filled with tears, but her chin remained aloft and she looked the others fully in the face. "I will return home and not force you into any awkwardness because of my actions."

"No," Alice said quickly. "You are our friend and we stick together. We will think of something to remedy this. Look at when Julia was in trouble, everyone rallied around and she was fine."

"She had not been rude to the most stringent of the patronesses," Serena said dryly. "I also do not have an earl supporting my cause."

"You have an earl-to-be," Alice said, looking hopefully at Hamish. Her heart sank when she saw his closed expression.

"I am not forcing anyone into marriage and scandal," Serena said before Hamish could speak. "Ben, do me one last favour, see me home. It seems I am to go on my Grand Tour after all."

"Oh Serena," Alice said as Ben and Serena left them without a look behind.

Chapter 20

The carriage ride home was a lot quieter than the outward journey. Hamish sat, looking out of the window, deep in thought, while Frances and Alice exchanged looks but could not speak openly whilst Hamish was with them.

As he was dropping them at Alice's door, he stepped out first and handed them out. While he held Alice's hand, he finally spoke. "I am sorry for everything tonight," he said, all laughter and funning gone.

"Why did you not speak up to protect her?" Alice asked.

"I was caught unawares, I just did not have time to think, but I will make it right," Hamish answered.

"I do not know how you can. She will be ostracised as far as society is concerned. Lady Jersey was probably the worst possible person to come across us."

"Somehow it will work out. I know I have obligations towards her."

"That is exactly why she reacted in the way she did," Alice said, exasperated. "None of us wants to marry out of obligation of any form. She was saving you both from a marriage that would end in you both being unhappy."

"There was no need for anyone to try to protect me," Hamish said. "She claimed that she was old enough to make her own decisions. Well, so am I."

Alice looked in surprise and a little suspicion at Hamish. "I hope in that case you make the right decisions."

"So do I. Miss Boyd, you must wish me to the devil at the moment, but could I possibly inconvenience you to accompany me to your publisher. Obviously, Miss Formby will be unable to join me as we had arranged."

Alice looked uncomfortable, but Frances spoke up. "If I could be the one to perform the introductions, it would be my pleasure, I have met Mr Mortimer a number of times, and I know Alice has a lot to do tomorrow."

"That would be of help to me," Alice said, feeling bad at letting Hamish and effectively Drew down, but she could not face Mr Mortimer just yet.

"Of course, thank you," Hamish said to Frances. "I will be leaving to see my brother tomorrow afternoon, so I shall take my leave of you now, Miss Boyd. I hope it will not be too long before we meet again."

"I hope so too," Alice said, refusing to let herself be filled with hope that he might convince James to give them another try. Hamish was just being polite, she chided herself and watched as the carriage drove away.

"Thank you for standing in for me," she said to Frances as they stepped through the front door of Alice's family house.

"I could see the look of horror in your eyes. I do not know Mr Mortimer as well as Serena, but he has hovered around so much that he will definitely know who I am, assuming he managed to take his eyes off you for a few minutes."

"Urgh, I hate upsetting people, and I know ultimately I am going to hurt him, and I am too cowardly to put the poor man out of his misery."

"You need to do it soon."

"I know, and I will."

***

Hamish collected Frances and they travelled in silence for a while. Frances was quiet by nature, and to be with a man who was clearly far more sophisticated than she was uncomfortable and intimidating.

After they had exchanged pleasantries, it was Hamish who broke the silence. "I am surprised but grateful that Miss Boyd's friends know her publisher."

"Yes, he has been in our company quite a lot since Alice's work was accepted by his company," Frances said.

"Is that usual?"

"I am afraid I do not know," Frances answered evasively.

"I see," Hamish responded, now even more curious to meet the publisher. He was no fool, he had seen the look of panic on Alice's face when he had asked her to accompany him. Both times her friends had stepped in, which was highly unusual. It was going to be an interesting morning.

Mr Mortimer was clearly surprised to see them but welcomed them into his office. There were piles of manuscripts on his desk, though the rest of the room was ordered. His bookshelves were filled with his authors that he readily pointed out to Hamish.

"This is a welcome diversion," he said, ordering tea from his clerk. "Sometimes reading manuscripts can be tedious, as the ones today are. If only there were a hundred Miss Boyds out there, my job would be far easier. I take it she is well?"

"Yes, she is just a little busy at the moment," Frances answered.

"I was surprised when she took a trip out of London recently to see her friend. It seemed rather sudden with everything going on."

"We are all keen to help our friends when they are in need, and she was soon home." Frances was almost squirming in her seat at the way Mr Mortimer was focused so much on Alice. She could see Hamish taking everything in by the tilt of his lips. "Mr Avril has brought some poetry which might just make your day better."

"Now I know all is well with Miss Boyd, my day has already improved. I hope to receive permission to call on her very soon. Ah, the tea is here. Shall I pour?"

"Please, allow me," Frances said. "Then you two can talk business." Unused to being forthright, she knew she had to try and focus Mr Mortimer on why they were there or he was likely to say even more that was inappropriate.

Hamish gave him the stack of papers which Drew had sent with him, and Mr Mortimer took his time in studying some of them. There were a lot of hmmms and ahhhhs as he read, which had Hamish and Frances glancing at each other while trying not to laugh.

Eventually, Mr Mortimer looked up at Hamish. "There is some merit in his work."

"Really?" Hamish asked, clearly incredulous.

"Yes. Some are a little too – let us just say shows a lack of worldly experience."

"That I can understand."

"I would only be willing to publish on commission," Mr Mortimer said. "A pamphlet of poetry we could try initially and see how that sells, then we can discuss further publications and different methods depending on sales."

"I see," Hamish said. "And how much will this venture cost my brother?"

"We usually sell poetry in a single volume, so it is not the same financial risk to him as if we were looking at a three-volume book. I will go through the rest of the poems and select the ones I think would be suitable, then we can either speak about costs or whether or not I feel we need more poems."

"That sounds reasonable," Hamish said. "Here is my card. I am leaving London this afternoon, but if you address any correspondence to Andrew Avril, my brother will receive your letter. Thank you for making a quick decision, I appreciate it."

"Oh, you can thank Miss Boyd for that," Mr Mortimer said, accepting the card. "Any friend who she recommends will always be seriously considered by myself, and I am happy to agree with her faith in your brother's writings."

"I see. Thank you for your time and your consideration. I shall inform my brother of what has passed today and that he should expect correspondence from yourself soon."

"Excellent, and if, Miss Somers, I could be so bold to ask you to pass on my sincerest regards to Miss Boyd, I would be very grateful."

"I will, of course," Frances said.

"I hope she approves of the flowers I send every day."

"I am sure she does," Francis replied. "They certainly fill the hallway."

"That gladdens my heart, for every time she leaves or enters her home, she must think of me," Mr Mortimer said, beaming at them both. "You have brightened my day considerably, Miss Somers. Thank you."

"I— Oh, good day, sir," Frances said as she was guided out by Hamish holding her arm and pulling her through the door.

They were silent until safely in the carriage, and Hamish leaned back with a laugh. "He should be writing novels with his flowery language," he blew out. "What a nodcock!"

"He is a little overwhelming," Frances acknowledged.

"Tell me, has he proposed already, or has Miss Boyd that pleasure to look forward to?"

"Oh. It is not for me to speak of private matters." Frances flushed with mortification, but she was no match for a man of the world. Saying nothing was almost as bad as saying too much, for Hamish was quick to pick up on everything.

"Ah, so he has already uttered the words. It makes sense that she is reluctant to see him. Why has she not just refused him? Surely she cannot like him?"

"Her brother has already had a disagreement with him over Mr Mortimer issuing thinly veiled threats that if he did not receive Alice's affections, he would no longer represent her." Frances finally gave in to trying to dodge the questions, at the back of her mind hoping it might do some good with Captain Avril if he found out Alice was being courted by another.

"Did he now? That is no way to run a business," Hamish murmured, his mind working quickly.

"Luckily, Mr Boyd had the sales figures for Alice's books and threatened to take her future work somewhere else. Apparently, Mr Mortimer soon apologised, but afterwards, her brother suggested that she might want to consider his proposal for Mr Mortimer would have her best interests at heart as it would be of benefit to them both if she were to marry her publisher."

"That is one way of looking at it, I suppose, although I would be astounded if she did not marry for love from the little I have seen of her. As for Mortimer, he clearly knows the ways of the publishing world, but he really needs to sharpen his skills in the area of charming women."

Frances sat in silence for a moment but then was compelled to speak, though her embarrassment was high. "I have to ask you, do you see charming a woman as some sort of sport? You seem to suggest it when referring to needing the skills to do it correctly."

Hamish laughed good-naturedly. He had seen his words had troubled her and was genuinely impressed that she had called him out on his gauche comment. "In some respects, it is a game when the romance or flirtation is not serious. I apologise for my brutish language, but can you not acknowledge that some of the women joining the marriage mart each season are trained in the finest of arts meant to ensnare a man as if they were on some sort of hunt?"

It was Frances's turn to snort with laughter. "You are completely right. I have been mortified at some of the actions I have seen over the years. It makes me ashamed to be a woman, but it sounds like men are just as contriving."

"Fortune hunters and the like can be, but when you meet someone who turns your head just for being themselves, well, in that case, the games suddenly stop." Hamish was serious as he spoke the words, and he looked out of the window.

"How are you going to make it right with Serena?" Frances asked, emboldened by their candid conversation.

"For the first time in my life, I am not sure what to do for the best. If you give me their direction, I can start by visiting Ben and Miss Formby."

"Oh, I do not think that would be a good idea," Frances said quickly.

"If I cannot contact either of them, how can I solve the issue of Miss Formby being ostracised and refusing to marry me?" Hamish asked with some understanding of Frances's protectiveness.

"Plants are far less complicated," Frances muttered to herself.

"I beg your pardon?" Hamish asked with a smile.

"Oh, blast. I really do need to stop thinking aloud. I was just saying that plants are a lot less complicated than people."

"I suppose they are, but there are plants that will poison you if not treated correctly," Hamish pointed out.

Frances smiled at him. "Yes, there are. Excuse my ramblings. I tend to avoid conversations unless I am with those who know my eccentric ways. I usually speak inappropriately."

"You have been a delightful companion today," Hamish said honestly. "And I do not please easily."

"Is this one of your skills to lull me into giving you Serena's address?"

Hamish laughed. "You have no need to worry about your own skills, Miss Somers. You are quite capable of matching anyone who would dare to try and bamboozle you, and believe me, that is a compliment."

"What you said was very flattering, but you did not actually answer my question," Frances pointed out, enjoying herself more than she could have imagined.

"My dear Miss Somers, you have my sincere regard. No, I did not utter the words in an effort to flatter you into giving me the address. I am hurt that you would think so."

"You are known as a rake, sir, though you are rarely in London. The gossip papers provide tittle-tattle from every major town. I cannot imagine my words having any effect of the kind on you."

"When I marry Miss Formby, I will be glad to be regularly in your company, Miss Somers, and if this is a hint of what your Bluestocking Club is like, then I cannot wait to meet the rest of you," Hamish said.

"We are here," Frances said, looking out the window at her home as the carriage came to a stop.

"Are you to help me, Miss Somers?" Hamish said, no longer the flirtatious rake.

"If you wait here, I will hurry inside and write Serena's details down."

"Thank you, I am very grateful."

"I am doing this for Serena," Frances said as she climbed out of the carriage. Returning moments later, she handed two pieces of paper to Hamish. "This is Serena's address, she lives with her parents, but her cousin has his own set of rooms. I cannot advise you which one to visit first, but I hope you choose wisely."

"So do I, Miss Somers. I can only try my hardest."

"Goodbye," Frances said, stepping back from the kerb.

She watched the carriage until it was out of sight, then turned and hurried back into her house. Her father was waiting for her in the hallway, a curious look on his face.

"Is there anything you wish to tell me, Frances?"

"No, Papa. I was hopefully helping a friend," Frances replied as she took off her bonnet and gloves.

"Ah, I thought with all the running about you were doing, there was some secret assignation being arranged."

Frances laughed. "Me? Papa, you know me too well to even think that. Although I have learned something interesting today."

"Enlighten me. I am always eager to hear about your discoveries," Mr Somers said.

"For once, it is not about plants," Frances said dryly. "I have discovered there are people – men – out there who might be happy to accept a woman as eccentric as I."

"I hate it when you speak so, child," Mr Somers said, his expression sad. "Of course there are men who will treasure you as you should be."

"I am not thinking of marriage. I am just thinking it would be nice to not feel so much an oddity sometimes."

Mr Somers put his arm around his daughter. "If anyone does not appreciate you for who you are, then they are a fool."

"Thank you, Papa, said like a completely biased parent," Frances smiled at him and received a kiss for her words.

Chapter 21

Hampshire – present day

When Hamish returned from his walk, he had calmed a little. He knew it was not purely to do with James that his temper was frayed, but he had to control himself, for now at least. Later he would sort out his own problems, for he had not managed to solve anything whilst in London. His first priority had to be James, for he could not stand by in all conscience and watch his brother throw his life away, which he would do if he entered another battlefield. Hamish had the perfect information to stir James into action, but he had to choose his moment.

Seeking out James on his return to the house, Hamish sat on the edge of James's bed. He shared a room with two other men, but they were away from their bedchamber, giving the brothers time to speak.

"I will come to London with you," Hamish said.

"There is no need. You will not talk me out of my decision," James said.

"I am not going to try." At the disbelieving look James aimed in Hamish's direction, Hamish laughed. "Not everything in the world revolves around you. I have my own business to attend to, and I wish to check on Miss Boyd. One of us should do so."

"Send her my regards," James said, walking over to the window.

Gritting his teeth at his brother's bloody-mindedness, Hamish tried to keep his voice calm, sitting on his hands because he felt the urge, yet again, to punch James. "I am more concerned about her safety."

James's head swung round to glare at Hamish. "Dinnae think you can fool me into galloping all the way to London on some Banbury story you have made up," he snapped. "I am no Johnny Raw."

"I never thought you were." Hamish shrugged, noticing that James had gripped the back of a chair. "I have already said my piece about you going on some fool's errand to fight someone else's battle. If I cannot dissuade you from that, I will be sad to lose you as a brother, but it is your decision, as it always has been. I am checking on Miss Boyd because if she is not careful, she will soon become Mrs Mortimer whether she likes it or not."

"Mortimer? Who is that? She is marrying?" James had flushed red, Hamish was not sure whether it was fear or anger, but at least it was a reaction.

"Mortimer is her publisher, and he has taken a very keen interest in Miss Boyd's personal situation as well as her professional one."

"The one to have put her before all others. His first choice," James said, once more looking out the window.

"It might be his first choice, but he is not hers," Hamish continued. "I could only coax a little information out of one of her friends, but it seems he is not beyond making threats to achieve his aim."

"What?!" James roared. "If he lays a finger on her, I will kill him."

"At last, the correct response." Hamish smiled. "She does not want him."

"Are you sure?" There was a vulnerability about James which belied his great form and his gruff mannerisms.

"Absolutely. She has her friends standing in for her; she looked afraid when I suggested she do the introductions, and I have not seen that expression on her before then. She tried to hide it, but you know well enough that I miss nothing."

"Aye, you are right there." James started pacing. "Why has her family not stepped in? I know she is close to them."

"Her brother took the publisher to task initially when he made some threat about not working with her if she did not do as he wished, but then her brother advised her to think of Mr Mortimer's proposal seriously. I suppose they think it would be the best offer she would receive, though he is of a different class," Hamish said. He was not going to put words in his brother's mouth, but he was constantly assessing when he could push and when he had to let James take the lead.

"The fool! She deserves more than someone who wants her for what money and respectability she brings to the match."

"Especially as she has become the pet of the Almack's patronesses, they are determined to make her the hit of the season."

"Then she will have even more proposals."

"Maybe," Hamish said. "I do not think she will accept any of them. She always seemed a little distracted to me, almost unhappy. Now don't you go sending me daggers with those eyes; I am speaking as I find."

"Pfftt."

"One thing I think you should consider..." Hamish knew his next words could go either way, and he could only hope that he had not miscalculated James's feelings at this point. "Being the blockhead that you are and a decent person who always does the right thing, you might want to consider if Mortimer was bold enough to make threats in the presence of Miss Boyd and her brother, what is he capable of if he manages to get her alone?"

"He would not dare," James said, teeth grinding.

"You have not met the man. I say he would if desperate enough and that day is rapidly approaching, going by the words he was uttering when I was in his company. He was being far too open about his feelings and wishes to someone who he had never met before. I do not know if it was some ploy to warn me off as a rival." There. Hamish could do no more.

"I will hang if he touches one hair on her head."

"How will you know? You are off to India in a few days."

"I am going to London now. Get the carriage ready; we have no time to lose. I am going to tell him exactly what he can and cannot do with regard to her." James started packing the few items he had while Hamish walked out to order the carriage.

Meeting Lydia in the hallway, he smiled at her.

"That is a smile full of mischief if ever I saw one," Lydia said.

"We are leaving immediately. For London. Or should I say to make sure Miss Boyd is safe from her dastardly publisher."

"I heard from Alice this morning; she is concerned that he is not going to take her refusal well," Lydia said.

"I am sure she had her reasons, but she really should have been firm with him from the start," Hamish said. "A man like that will not likely be hinted away."

"Her insecurities about her career as an author have probably had a lot to do with how she hesitated in being firm with him. I know she can stand up for herself, but in this case, she feels like it is her only chance to be successful, so she is being more hesitant than she would be normally."

"From the way it was described to me how quickly Mortimer backed down when challenged about not working with her, I would say she has no worries about her future."

"Is the carriage here?" James demanded, thundering down the stairs. "We need to be on our way."

"That, Lady Fleetwood, seems to be my cue to depart," Hamish said with a bow. "Thank you for all you have done for my brother. You deserve a medal."

James paused. "Thank you. For everything and more. I was furious when you sent for Miss Boyd, but you were right. She was the only one who could demand I sorted myself out and live to tell the tale."

Lydia burst out laughing. "I know, which is why I sent for her. I hope you have a good journey. Be kind to Alice; she has been under a lot of pressure."

"Do ye have to tell everyone everything," James shot at Hamish.

"As if she did not know already." Hamish grinned. "Come on, chattering brother, the carriage is waiting."

"My lady, you do more good than you can ever imagine. I am very thankful that you took me in. Twice," James said quietly.

"That is very kind of you. Now go!" Lydia said, almost pushing him out of the door. "And only come back if you have a wife to bring," she said quietly, but the wink she received from Hamish as he stepped in the coach was all the reassurance she needed.

***

London

Alice paced the morning room, hands twisting almost as much as her stomach was. This was it. When the knocker on the door sounded, she would have to face him and be honest and forceful. She would normally consider herself quietly confident, but there was something about Mr Mortimer that had unnerved her from the start. The contracts were already written by the time she met him, and she had not wished to cause problems when her books were so close to being published, but the way he looked at her had made her skin crawl.

Knowing that she had been unfair in keeping his hopes alive, she had sent a letter to his place of business and asked that he join her this morning. It had seemed like a good idea to have the visit take place when her mother was out visiting, but now she felt exposed and vulnerable.

Trying to settle her nerves, she cursed herself. The house was full of servants; one scream would bring them all. Of course, she was not alone, though she felt it.

Hearing the knocker did nothing to ease her tension. Putting her hand on her stomach, she tried to calm her breathing, or she was certain she would faint.

The footman announced Mr Mortimer, and all too soon the gentleman was standing before her. Ordering tea to be brought, when she really wanted brandy, she invited him to sit.

"I was so glad to have received your message," Mr Mortimer said. "It has been too long since we saw each other. I know you asked for time to consider everything, but I had not thought it needed quite so much thought."

There was the hint of a whine in his voice, which made Alice sit a little straighter. "I am sorry about that, but my family and friends urged me to think over your proposal carefully, as it would change my circumstances considerably."

A blush creeping up his neck, Mr Mortimer visibly seethed. "I know I am considered lower than the gentry by earning my living, but I would point out that their lives would be far more tedious if I did not provide the service I do. You obviously have issues with my being a tradesman, which I am surprised about."

"No! Not at all," Alice rushed. "I do not think in that way; you misunderstand my meaning. They meant that I would have to consider no longer writing."

"Why?"

"Because I would be keeping house and raising a family."

"We would have enough staff that you could still write," Mr Mortimer said, relaxing a little.

The maid interrupted, bringing a heavily laden tea tray. Waiting until she had left them once more, though leaving the door open, Alice took a few moments respite in fussing with the tea and offering cakes.

When they both had full plates and cups, which neither was touching, Alice set her shoulders. "I thank you for your proposal, Mr Mortimer. I am very grateful that you would consider me for your wife, but I am afraid I cannot accept."

Jumping to his feet, Mortimer knocked the plate of cakes onto the floor. Without even glancing at it, he stepped to the fire and banged his fist on the mantlepiece. "And that is it? I wait weeks to then be brought in, offered a bit of cake and refused?"

"I am sorry, truly I am, but I could not think of another way of telling you the news. I did not think it was fair to write you a letter."

"You could have said no the moment I asked you."

"I genuinely considered your offer," Alice defended herself.

"But it is a no."

"I am afraid so."

"All the time and money I have invested in you, and you are casting me aside, like a nobody?"

"I never asked for anything other than what you would have given any other author!" Alice was furious at the accusation but tried to remain calm. It would not do to lose her temper, but his words made her wish him miles away.

"Did you not? All the *oh thank you, Mr Mortimer, you are so kind, so helpful to little old me, what would I do without you*," he responded in a mocking tone.

"I do thank you for all you have done for me with regards to the publishing of the books, but you have benefited from your efforts too," Alice said. "I never asked or looked for affection from you at any time."

"Because you think you are above everyone else," he snarled at her.

Alice jumped to her feet, no longer able to contain her annoyance. "I do not!" she snapped. "I am probably the one who feels less important than most people, but that does not mean to say that I will agree to marry a man I do not love and could never hold in affection."

Mortimer had swung around to face Alice, and he stepped forward. "Love? Love? I would have worshipped the ground you walked on, whether you cared for me or not. I was prepared to earn your love, to marry you though I could offer you so much, and you have turned me down as if none of what I offered was good enough." He had taken a step towards Alice, and she instinctively stepped back. "You really do not like me, do you?" he laughed, spittle hitting her in the face.

Wiping her face with the back of her hand, Alice stood as tall as she could, but Mortimer towered over her. Cursing her lack of height, she hoped her expression and tone of voice made up for it. "Of course it was good enough, you foolish man! That is why I have thought about it, but I cannot enter a marriage when we are not equal, not in class before you start to rant about that again, but with regards to affection. I could never learn to love you when my heart is full of another."

"You are playing with someone else's emotions. Are you trying to see who makes the best offer? Has he more money? A bigger house?" Mortimer spat.

"No! He has not made me an offer." Technically he had, but after the debacle with Constance it had been rescinded.

Mortimer laughed. "You are hanging around in the hope he will? A bluestocking who is beyond her prime and should be thankful she has received one proposal. The problem I have now is that I have decided that you are going to be my wife, and when I make my mind up about something, I always get my own way."

"Not in this instance, you will not. I am not going to marry you," Alice said, hands on hips. "In fact, I want you to leave."

"Leave a room in which we are alone? Leave at the very moment I am going to compromise you in order that you cannot avoid a union with me? Oh no, I am not about to go meekly, Miss Boyd. The time for that has passed."

Mortimer grabbed her by the arms and started to pull her towards him, his lips were puckered, and Alice thought she was going to cast up her accounts, but instead she brought her knee up and delivered a well-aimed shot.

Screaming out in surprise, Mortimer bent double, and Alice punched him in the eye before pushing him backwards. The tea tray and everything on it went tumbling to the floor as the table collapsed under the weight of her attacker.

Moving out of his reach, she prepared to run from the room, but looking up, she almost collapsed with relief when she saw James and Hamish standing in the doorway.

"James was going to burst in and save the day, but it seems you have things fully under control, Miss Boyd. I have to say, you were mighty impressive," Hamish drawled.

"Thank you," Alice said shakily. "My friend Julia taught us a few moves to protect ourselves should the need arise, but I can honestly say that even punching the eye hurts terribly. I do not think I will be writing for days."

James had never taken his eyes off Alice but did not say a word until he let out a battle cry when Mortimer suddenly lunged at her. Mortimer managed to knock her onto a sofa but was then roughly dragged away.

"I will ruin you for this!" he spat at Alice as James marched him to the door.

Hamish stepped aside to let the pair out but looked at Mr Mortimer. "If one word of this gets out, my brother and I will make sure that every gossip paper, every newspaper, knows how you conduct business. I would imagine that your clientele would soon dry up when they know how you treat defenceless young women."

"Damn you!" Mr Mortimer snarled.

"I would not be worried about me. I would be very concerned about my brother who is holding you up. You see, he is the one who is in love with Miss Boyd, and he does not take kindly to anyone he loves being misused. I do hope you have the services of a good doctor, for you are going to need one." With his words, Hamish stepped into the room and closed the door on James and Mortimer.

Alice tried to stand, but Hamish immediately approached her and laid his hand on her arm. "He will not kill him, just let James give him his just desserts," he said soothingly. "I do not suppose you have brandy in this room, do you?"

"My father always keeps some in the cabinet next to the window," Alice answered. "Could I have a glass too, please? And as for giving him his just desserts, I did not think I was doing too badly myself."

"Oh, you were wonderful to watch," Hamish said conversationally, though there was the sound of a serious fight going on in the hallway. "But I have to say that James would have probably exploded if he had not had the opportunity to vent his anger on the man who was not playing fair with you."

"Gallant as always," Alice said with a note of bitterness.

"I am glad we have a moment to ourselves," Hamish said as another thud was heard. "I need to tell you something, and I am being perfectly serious."

"Go on."

"My foolish brother is hurting so much and feeling that you deserve better than him that he is about to sign up with the East India Company and go to India to suppress the locals," Hamish said. "I know without a doubt that the first skirmish he is involved with, he will get himself killed because without you in his life, he feels he has lost everything."

"He only needs to ask," Alice said through gritted teeth.

"I know that, and you know that, but as I have already told him, he is a blockhead and more so when you are involved. Selfishly, I do not want to see my brother killed, but I also would be more than happy if he married you."

"What can I do if he will not see sense?"

"I am sure you will think of something."

"I am glad you have confidence in me," Alice said dryly.

"Oh, and did I mention that you probably only have the rest of the day to do it? He was coming to London tomorrow to sign up until I managed to persuade him that Mortimer could not be trusted to take your rejection like a gentleman."

"Wonderful."

"That is plenty of time, for I keep being told that you are the only one who can handle my brother to look after his best interests, and in this case, it will save his life and marry him off. If you are as good as I think," Hamish smiled.

"I think I need another brandy," Alice said, handing him her empty glass.

Chapter 22

Hamish eventually left the room, and with the help of the footmen, they split up the fight. Mortimer had given up trying to retaliate and was just avoiding James as much as possible. When the pair were separated, Hamish looked at his brother.

"I will deposit this fool at his address. I suggest you check on Miss Boyd's hand. Joking aside, we do not want her hand to be permanently damaged, for she has genuine talent."

James nodded and looked at one of the footmen. "Bring ice to Miss Boyd and towels, and I do not care who calls; she is not at home."

"Yes, sir," the terrified footman said.

Walking into the morning room, James noticed Alice was holding her glass with her left hand, not her right and immediately crossed to her. "You are hurt," he said, kneeling before her.

"I am finding two glasses of brandy is helping the pain. Did you win?" Alice asked, a little tipsy smile on her lips.

"I am insulted that you even have to ask that question," James responded with his usual glower as he examined her hand.

The footman knocked and brought the towels and ice as commanded, putting it down on the occasional table next to James.

"Oh, George, could you please pass me the decanter? I think I need more brandy," Alice said.

"I think you have had enough," James growled.

"Do not be a spoilsport. I have been through a lot today. I should be swooning on the sofa now, but I think I will recommend brandy to anyone in future as it is far more pleasant than smelling salts. Have you ever sniffed them? They are vile," Alice gabbled, completely unused to the large glasses full of alcohol Hamish had given her.

"I have not," James said, examining Alice's hand and positioning the ice, wrapped in a towel over her knuckles and holding it in place. She winced, and he nodded to the footman. "Give her a small glass," he instructed. "And then leave."

The footman looked relieved if a little guilty at leaving Alice with the ruffian, but as he had just witnessed what the man could do with his fists, he was not about to argue.

"This is nice. You here with me, holding my hand and me drinking brandy. I thought today was going to be awful, but I am actually very happy." Alice smiled at him.

"Eh, lassie, what am I going to do with you?" James said, smiling softly at her.

"You do not need to do anything, I am surprised Gentleman Jackson is not knocking on the door, inviting me to join him in the ring. Whenever you get involved in a fight, just send for me, and I will sort it."

"I will keep that in mind."

"There is something I should be doing, but I cannot quite think what it is. Do you know?"

"No. I think you have done enough today."

Alice drained her glass and slammed it down on the table, nearly missing it. "I remember! I have to marry you!"

"What?" James reared back on his haunches.

"That is it. You are here, and Mr Mortimer is gone, and we can get married." Alice stood, and although James tried to keep the ice on her knuckles, she pushed it off. "You are silly."

"That is fine talk coming from you," James said, watching her warily. "You are foxed."

"Am I? I have never been foxed before." Alice grinned, leaning forward and putting her hands on his shoulders as she was taller than him. "I would highly recommend it."

"You might feel different in the morning when you wake with the worst headache you have ever had."

"Will you be with me?"

James took hold of her hands and gently forced her to sit down. "I cannot spend the night with you; the brandy has made you lose your sense of reason." Putting some distance between them, he sat down in a chair opposite her. He wanted to remain close by in case she was in danger of hurting herself, but for his own sanity, he needed to be apart from her.

"You stayed with me when I had a headache last time," Alice pouted.

Nearly groaning with the need to kiss her, James rubbed his hands through his hair before sitting on them to stop himself from acting on his impulse. "That was different."

"It was not. I was sad then. I am sad now."

"You just said you were happy."

"That was when I was touching you. I am sad when you are not near me."

"Blast it, woman, why are you torturing us this way? I cannot wait until tomorrow, then I can be sane again."

"Tomorrow. There is something about tomorrow that I do not like," Alice mused, her finger on her lips as she pondered. James knew the instant she remembered what she was thinking of, for she jumped to her feet. "Oh no you do not, Captain Avril! I refuse to stand by and let you do it, if not for my sake, for Hamish."

"You are rambling." He was watching her more warily.

Alice started to pace. "Hamish is right. You are a blockhead."

"Thank you."

"Stop interrupting. I cannot think straight."

"You surprise me."

Alice glared at him, which made him laugh, and he shrugged at her until she was satisfied that he was not going to speak again. "I will not let you get yourself killed. It would upset Hamish, and I would be a little sad too."

"A little?" James could not help asking.

"Maybe a lot," Alice said, looking at him sternly. "Why will you not marry me?"

"You deserve better than me."

"I hate it when people think they know what is best for me, do you not?"

"I suppose so."

"My brother said a marriage to Mr Mortimer would secure my future but the thought of laying with him..." She shuddered but looked in surprise as James jumped to his feet at her words. "I could not do it. I would always be thinking of you."

"Good God, woman! You definitely were sent to torture me." He turned away from her, knowing his resolve was disappearing at the thought of her with someone else.

Alice approached him and wrapped her arms around his middle, her head on his back. "I love how my hands do not reach around you."

"Are you suggesting that I am fat?" he grumbled.

"No. I think you are perfect in every way, apart from when you are being a blockhead, of course." James swung around, keeping hold of her arms. Alice looked surprised at his sudden movement, but she smiled at him. "Kiss me, you big oaf."

Unable to withstand her words, James took her into his arms and kissed her as he had wanted to for weeks. His hands roamed across her back, messing with her hair, pulling clips out and throwing them on the floor. Growling with pleasure as her blonde curls tumbled around her face, he cupped her face gently in his hands.

"I always feel like an unwieldy brute when I am around you," he said, kissing her with reverence.

"I love your size, your eyes, your smile, your frowns and especially your kisses," Alice whispered. "Promise not to stop kissing me."

Taking her back into his arms, he took his time, kissing her without the initial urgency he had felt, but the kisses were no less intense.

Resting his forehead on hers, he smiled at her. "I love everything about you, lassie," he whispered.

"Please do not leave me. I do not think I could stand it, however much that makes me sound like Drew," Alice said quietly.

"I should go and let you have the life you deserve, with all the fine things in the world," James said, knowing full well that nothing would separate him from her after the afternoon they had shared.

"Can I not be the one who decides what is best for me? I want to live in the Highlands with my brutish husband, the one I am able to bully into doing whatever I wish because he is the most wonderful man I have ever known."

"You make it sound perfect," James said, kissing her gently.

"What on earth is going on here? And why are there two tables broken in the hallway?" Mrs Boyd demanded as she stood in the doorway, her husband by her side.

"Mrs Boyd, I apologise and will pay for replacements," James said, trying to move away from Alice, but she clung to him.

"Mama, I think I have managed to persuade James – that is, oh dear, I think I am going to cast up my accounts."

And she did.

***

Alice groaned as she opened her eyes. "I never want to taste brandy again." She moaned as the thought of it made her stomach roil.

"I am glad to hear it," James responded.

Opening her eyes and trying to sit up at the sound of his voice, she lay back with a whimper, not helped by the chuckle she heard from James. Sighing in relief when he placed a cold cloth on her forehead, she kept her eyes closed until the extreme banging in her head eased a little.

"Have some water, it will help," James said, moving around and gently lifting her up so she could drink.

"What are you doing in my chamber, and where are my parents? I do not remember much, but I will never forget the look on my mother's face when she interrupted us."

"You missed the look of horror she gave you when you decided that there was a need for a new carpet."

"Ohhh," Alice groaned. "I was ill all over the carpet?"

"Very ill." James was smiling, but Alice could not quite meet his gaze.

"You must think I am awful."

"Not at all. You always seem to be able to bring me to my senses and make me laugh, even when you are completely embarrassed and cursing yourself to the devil. I think your mother will wish to speak to you about the language you were using. I have told her this trait of yours has nothing to do with me."

"Brute!" Alice said, finally looking at him. The effect was as intense as the last time he had held her so gently when she had been injured. His blue eyes bore into her, and she hoped as she had never allowed herself to hope since leaving Scotland. "Tell me if I have a chance with you," she said quietly. "I need to know now if I am to lose you again."

James smiled at her. "No, you are not going to lose me ever again. I have sent a message home to say that I am well and happy, and the next time they see me, I will be married."

Once more, Alice tried to sit up, and though her head pounded, she managed to kneel up and gripped his waistcoat. "Are you being serious?"

"Of course I am, but you are preventing me from making the romantic proposal you wanted from me," James said, laughing.

"You want to marry me? Nothing will change your mind?" Alice was almost shaking him.

"I want to no matter what, although if I did not feel that way, I think your parents would have something to say about the matter after discovering us in the morning room."

"You do not need to marry me out of obligation," Alice said, her expression falling a little.

James grabbed her hands and twisted so that she was lying underneath him. "I have wanted you since the first moment I set eyes on you. I wanted to marry you, ravish you and laugh with you all at the same time. I have been the blockhead both you and Hamish accused me of, but no more. We are to marry by special licence, which your father is arranging, so get rid of any foolish notions, for you have had my love, my heart, my soul since the moment I saw you."

"Those are the most romantic words I have ever heard," Alice said, her face lighting up with happiness, all thoughts of headaches gone.

"Thank goodness for that!" James said, flopping to the side of her so their heads were next to each other on the pillows. It was intimate, and he had never felt more content in his life. "I do hope your father can arrange everything quickly."

"Me too. There is just one thing," Alice said, a mischievous smile on her lips.

"Anything, lassie."

"Are you going to wear your kilt at the wedding?"

"Yes, and you will be able to think throughout the service that you have already seen what is underneath!" Alice started laughing, her hands over her burning cheeks and was wrapped in an embrace. James kissed the top of the head.

"I will blush throughout the service now, you oaf," Alice chastised, still chuckling.

"Good, for I will be as nervous as a green boy until we are wed."

Alice touched his face. "There is no need to be worried, I will be there every step of the way with you."

"That is all I could ever wish for," James said. "I am so glad I met you, lassie. I will always treasure my kilt for being the catalyst that brought us together."

"Me too, but I will appreciate the man more," Alice said, kissing her soon-to-be husband in a way that would have the patronesses despairing that their protégée was acting so outrageously.

Luckily for Alice, the Highlands of Scotland were about as far from Almack's as one could get, so she could kiss and be kissed with abandon.

The end

Read Serena and Hamish's story in The Bluestocking's Rake:-

https://www.amazon.com/dp/B0BMB45Y3W

https://www.amazon.co.uk/dp/B0BMB45Y3W

https://www.amazon.de/dp/B0BMB45Y3W

https://www.amazon.ca/dp/B0BMB45Y3W

https://www.amazon.com.au/dp/B0BMB45Y3W

About the Author

I have had the fortune to live a dream. I've always wanted to write, but life got in the way as it so often does until a few years ago. Then a change in circumstance enabled me to do what I loved: sit down to write. Now writing has taken over my life, holidays being based around research, so much so that no matter where we go, my long-suffering husband says, 'And what connection to the Regency period has this building/town/garden got?'

That dream became a little more surreal when in 2018, I became an Amazon StorytellerUK Finalist with Lord Livesey's Bluestocking. A Regency Romance in the top five of an all-genre competition! It was a truly wonderful experience, I didn't expect to win, but I had a ball at the awards ceremony.

I do appreciate it when readers get in touch, especially if they love the characters as much as I do. Those first few weeks after release is a trying time; I desperately want everyone to love my characters that take months and months of work to bring to life.

If you enjoy the books please would you take the time to write a review on Amazon? Reviews are vital for an author who is just starting out, although I admit to bad ones being crushing. Selfishly I want readers to love my stories!

I can be contacted for any comments you may have, via my website: www.audreyharrison.co.uk or www.facebook.com/AudreyHarrisonAuthor

Please sign-up for email/newsletter – only sent out when there is something to say.

www.audreyharrison.co.uk

You'll receive a free copy of The Unwilling Earl in mobi/epub format for signing-up as a thank you!

Novels by Audrey Harrison

Regency Romances – newest release first

The Bluestocking's Quest – The Bluestocking Club – book 1
https://www.amazon.com/dp/B09YPKCLNX
https://www.amazon.co.uk/dp/B09YPKCLNX
The Bluestocking's Fortune – The Bluestocking Club – Book 2
https://www.amazon.com/dp/B09YML7MS3
https://www.amazon.co.uk/dp/B09YML7MS3
The Spinster's Captain – The Spinster Series – book 1
https://www.amazon.com/dp/B096BDHXBF
https://www.amazon.co.uk/dp/B096BDHXBF
The Spinster's Second Chance – the Spinster Series – book 2
https://www.amazon.com/dp/B09671D13F
https://www.amazon.co.uk/dp/B09671D13F
The American Spinster – The Spinster Series – Book 3
https://www.amazon.com/dp/B09LHQ13N4
https://www.amazon.co.uk/dp/B09LHQ13N4
Book bundle – **A Trilogy of Trouble**
https://www.amazon.com/dp/B09NL62SB9
https://www.amazon.co.uk/dp/B09NL62SB9
The Colonel's Spinster
https://www.amazon.com/dp/B08N1K9Y4H
https://www.amazon.co.uk/dp/B08N1K9Y4H

Lady Edith's Lonely Heart – The Lonely Hearts Series – book 1
https://www.amazon.com/dp/B0852RMGJJ
https://www.amazon.co.uk/dp/B0852RMGJJ
Miss King's Rescue – The Lonely Hearts Series – book 2
https://www.amazon.com/dp/B08778RJQP
https://www.amazon.co.uk/dp/B08778RJQP
Captain Jones's Temptation – The Lonely Hearts Series – book 3
https://www.amazon.com/dp/B08775663R
https://www.amazon.co.uk/dp/B08775663R
The Lonely Lord
https://www.amazon.com/dp/B07S1X5NBZ
https://www.amazon.co.uk/dp/B07S1X5NBZ
The Drummond Series:-
Lady Lou the Highwayman – Drummond series Book 1
https://www.amazon.com/dp/B07NDX3HV2
https://www.amazon.co.uk/dp/B07NDX3HV2
Saving Captain Drummond – Drummond Series Book 2
https://www.amazon.com/dp/B07NFBRZFG
https://www.amazon.co.uk/dp/B07NFBRZFG
Book bundle – **The Drummonds**
https://www.amazon.com/dp/B08TVYYBZY
https://www.amazon.co.uk/dp/B08TVYYBZY
Lord Livesey's Bluestocking (Amazon Storyteller Finalist 2018)
https://www.amazon.com/dp/B07D3T6L93
https://www.amazon.co.uk/dp/B07D3T6L93
Return to the Regency – A Regency Time-travel novel
https://www.amazon.com/dp/B078C87HVX
https://www.amazon.co.uk/dp/B078C87HVX
My Foundlings:-
The Foundling Duke – The Foundlings Book 1
https://www.amazon.com/dp/B071KTT9CD

https://www.amazon.co.uk/dp/B071KTT9CD

The Foundling Lady – The Foundlings Book 2

https://www.amazon.com/dp/B072L2D7PF

https://www.amazon.co.uk/dp/B072L2D7PF

Book bundle – **The Foundlings**

https://www.amazon.com/dp/B07Q6YLND4

https://www.amazon.co.uk/dp/B07Q6YLND4

Mr Bailey's Lady

https://www.amazon.com/dp/B01NACMFVJ

https://www.amazon.co.uk/dp/B01NACMFVJ

The Spy Series:-

My Lord the Spy

https://www.amazon.com/dp/B01F11ZRM8

https://www.amazon.co.uk/dp/B01F11ZRM8

My Earl the Spy

https://www.amazon.com/dp/B01F12NG8E

https://www.amazon.co.uk/dp/B01F12NG8E

Book bundle – **The Spying Lords**

https://www.amazon.com/dp/B07RV3JQFP

https://www.amazon.co.uk/dp/B07RV3JQFP

The Captain's Wallflower

https://www.amazon.com/dp/B018PDBGLK

https://www.amazon.co.uk/dp/B018PDBGLK

The Four Sisters' Series:-

Rosalind – Book 1

https://www.amazon.com/dp/B00WWTXSA6

https://www.amazon.co.uk/dp/B00WWTXSA6

Annabelle – Book 2

https://www.amazon.com/dp/B00WWTXRWA

https://www.amazon.co.uk/dp/B00WWTXRWA

Grace – Book 3

https://www.amazon.com/dp/B00WWUBEWO

https://www.amazon.co.uk/dp/B00WWUBEWO

Eleanor – Book 4

https://www.amazon.com/dp/B00WWUBF1E
https://www.amazon.co.uk/dp/B00WWUBF1E
Book Bundle – **The Four Sisters**
https://www.amazon.com/dp/B01416W0C4
https://www.amazon.co.uk/dp/B01416W0C4
The Inconvenient Trilogy:-
The Inconvenient Ward – Book 1
https://www.amazon.com/dp/B00KCJUJFA
https://www.amazon.co.uk/dp/B00KCJUJFA
The Inconvenient Wife – Book 2
https://www.amazon.com/dp/B00KCJVQU2
https://www.amazon.co.uk/dp/B00KCJVQU2
The Inconvenient Companion – Book 3
https://www.amazon.com/dp/B00KCK87T4
https://www.amazon.co.uk/dp/B00KCK87T4
Book bundle – **An Inconvenient Trilogy**
https://www.amazon.com/dp/B00PHQIZ18
https://www.amazon.co.uk/dp/B00PHQIZ18
The Complicated Earl
https://www.amazon.com/dp/B00BCN90DC
https://www.amazon.co.uk/dp/B00BCN90DC
The Unwilling Earl (Novella)
https://www.amazon.com/dp/B00BCNE2HG
https://www.amazon.co.uk/dp/B00BCNE2HG

Other Eras
A Very Modern Lord
Years Apart

Printed in Great Britain
by Amazon

39532384R00146